"PHILADELPHIA . . ."

"You can call me Jane."

B.J. couldn't bring herself to remove her hand from his cheek. Slowly the tip of her tongue flicked out and licked her bottom lip.

"Is that your name?"

"My sister calls me that sometimes. When she really wants to get my attention."

Crash's intense scrutiny made her shiver.

"I really want to get your attention."

He shifted toward her, not so much a shifting of body as a shifting of soul. It was a subtle change that shone through his eyes. She knew then that he was going to kiss her, just as she knew that it would be the kind of kiss a woman never forgets, the kind that imprints on the heart as surely as it imprints on the mind.

The kiss was tender beyond imagining, lush and warm and full of all the things a woman dreams, so tender she almost cried. Outside her tent the rain pattered steadily against canvas, a hypnotic almost ethereal rhythm that blurred time and place. Cradled in Crash's arms she felt cozy and warm and safe, far removed from the trials of everyday living.

Don't let me make a fool of myself, she thought, but she was already beyond reason, completely lost in the magic of the kiss.

WHAT ARE *LOVESWEPT* ROMANCES?

They are stories of true romance and touching emotion. We believe those two very important ingredients are constants in our highly sensual and very believable stories in the LOVE-SWEPT line. Our goal is to give you, the reader, stories of consistently high quality that may sometimes make you laugh, sometimes make you cry, but are always fresh and creative and contain many delightful surprises within their pages.

Most romance fans read an enormous number of books. Those they truly love, they keep. Others may be traded with friends and soon forgotten. We hope that each LOVESWEPT romance will be a treasure—a "keeper." We will always try to publish

LOVE STORIES YOU'LL NEVER FORGET
BY AUTHORS YOU'LL ALWAYS REMEMBER

The Editors

Loveswept® 847

BRINGING UP BAXTER

PEGGY WEBB

BANTAM BOOKS
NEW YORK · TORONTO · LONDON · SYDNEY · AUCKLAND

BRINGING UP BAXTER

A Bantam Book / August 1997

ISBN 0-553-44618-5

Published simultaneously in the United States and Canada

Bantam Books are published by Bantam Books, a division of Bantam
Doubleday Dell Publishing Group, Inc. Its trademark, consisting of the
words "Bantam Books" and the portrayal of a rooster, is Registered in U.S.
Patent and Trademark Office and in other countries. Marca Registrada.
Bantam Books, 1540 Broadway, New York, New York 10036.

PRINTED IN THE UNITED STATES OF AMERICA
OPM   10 9 8 7 6 5 4 3 2 1

ONE

B. J. slid the knife through the tape as carefully as if she were dissecting a frog. The cardboard box parted and she took out a fat volume, *Criminal Law, Second Edition*, LaFave and Scott, then carried it to the shelves with the same precise movements she'd used in opening the box.

In control. That's what she was.

"B. J.," her sister called from the next room. "Come in here and see this. It's gorgeous."

B. J. looked at the huge stack of boxes, the wall of empty shelves, the curtainless windows at the end of a large empty room. A million tasks needed her attention.

"I'm busy, Maxie."

She took another book from her box then checked it off her list. A tousle of red curls appeared around the doorframe, followed by her sister's paint-spattered face.

"Come *on*, B. J." Maxie swept into the room, trailing paintbrushes, wallpaper borders, and the scent of jungle gardenia. "You've got to see this."

Maxie grabbed her arm and propelled her down the paneled hallway into the spacious front room.

"Ta-da!" Maxie made a sweeping gesture.

"My God. It's red." B. J. put her hand over her throat. "Maxie . . . you've painted the walls *red*."

"I know. I figured the people who come to you could use some perking up. Do you like it?"

"When I told you to paint any color you wanted, I never dreamed you'd choose red. . . . I think I'm going to have to sit down."

What would soon become the law offices of B. J. Corban, formerly of a ritzy address in Philadelphia but lately of her sister's modest address in Tupelo, Mississippi, was now only an unfurnished, partially painted 1950s house on Broadway Street. B. J. sat on the floor.

"You don't like it?"

"I didn't say that, Maxie."

"You didn't have to. I can tell by the way you squint your eyes and scrunch up your mouth when you don't like something."

"You make me sound like a dried up old prune."

Which wasn't far from the truth. Otherwise, why would she be sitting on a dusty floor in Tupelo with her sister, while Stephen Matthews III combed the beaches of St. Croix and St. Thomas with another woman? A younger woman, at that. And on B. J.'s honeymoon.

B. J. jumped up and grabbed the first thing she

could get her hands on, a roll of wallpaper and a pot of paste.

"Hey . . . I didn't mean to upset you."

"I'm not upset."

"Then why are you pasting the wallpaper border on the door?"

The solid oak door, ancient and sturdy, now sported a precise border of stalking tigers, tigers that bore a striking resemblance to Stephen Matthews, who knew more about prowling than any man in Philadelphia.

"Linda's pregnant," he'd told B. J. as he stood at the back of All Saints Episcopal with a red rose pinned to his tuxedo.

"Stephen, this is no time for practical jokes," B. J. had said, never even pausing as she adjusted her veil. Then, she'd seen his face in the mirror. "Who is Linda?"

"The girl I'm going to marry."

The girl he *had* married, the girl who would soon be sitting in the house B. J. had designed, on the very sofa B. J. had picked out. She raked at the wallpaper on her door as if it were Stephen's face.

"Here, let me do that." Maxie attacked the border with a bucket of water and a scrub brush.

"I don't need any help. I'm in perfect control of the situation."

"I know you are." Maxie kept on scrubbing.

"Why wouldn't I be? All Philadelphia knows that B. J. Corban always wins. According to all the newspapers, I'm the most brilliant orator since Clarence Darrow."

She tossed a wad of ruined wallpaper in the general direction of the wastebasket, and missed. The sticky glob spatted onto the hardwood floor. On her hands and knees, B. J. cleaned up the mess.

"Of course Clarence Darrow wasn't female. Nobody ever left him stranded at the altar with his biological clock ticking. Nobody ever courted him for five years, then married somebody half his age. Nobody ever told him he knew plenty about torts but nothing about romance."

The last word came out a wail, and B. J. swiped at her face with the back of her sticky hand.

"Here, take this." Maxie pulled a rumpled tissue from the back pocket of her jeans.

"I'm not crying."

"In case you do."

B. J. grabbed the tissue and honked her nose. "I just need to get back to work, that's all."

"What you need is a change of scene."

"What do you call this?" B. J. made the same sweeping gesture her sister had used earlier. "Chopped liver?"

Suddenly B. J. was daunted. Thirty-eight and starting over. And all because she couldn't bear to have the close-knit society of Philadelphia blue bloods know that B. J. Corban was not, after all, a winner. The unflattering truth was that she'd turned tail and run. Betty Jane, the Corban sister with all the potential, the one who had left and carved out a brilliant career, had skulked back home like a whipped chicken.

"I'm not talking about work," Maxie said. "You need to go someplace and play."

"I'll leave that to the Stephen Matthewses of the world."

When Maxie got an idea she wouldn't let go. Wearing blue baby doll pajamas and purple nail polish, curled into a pink plush chair in her small yellow house on Maxwell Street with the moon shining through the window on her cap of red curls, she looked like an angel instead of what she was: the most stubborn woman on earth.

"Listen to this." Bent over the magazine in her lap called *Great Getaways*, she read aloud, " 'Montana Hideaway. Dine under the stars, rope steers, ride cowboys.' "

"I think you mean, ride *with* cowboys." B. J. tucked her bare feet under her, smoothed an imaginary wrinkle from her plain white sleepshirt, then leaned back on Maxie's flowered chintz sofa.

"On the other hand, you probably didn't." Her sister's wicked grin told her all she needed to know. "Look, Maxie. I'm not going anywhere except to that lumpy mattress in your guest bedroom. Tomorrow I've got to start looking for a house."

"How about this one? 'Smoky Mountains Retreat, camp under the stars, hike in the woods, fish for rainbow trout.' "

"Sounds like something Marlin Perkins would love. For Pete's sake, Maxie, give it a rest. Can you picture me trekking through the woods in my three-piece suit and my black pumps?"

Her shoes weren't black pumps: they were brand-new Nike's, and they'd already rubbed a blister. If B. J. ever got home, she swore she was going to kill Maxie.

She limped to her car and struggled to get the tent—the best money could buy the enthusiastic muscle-bound salesman at the sporting goods store had told her—out of her trunk. Everything B. J. had purchased for her getaway in the Smokies was the best money could buy. Even the hiking shorts with all the zippered pockets.

"For keeping things," the clerk had said when B. J. asked.

"What things?"

"Compass, maps, rations, hunting knives."

"Good grief. Hunting knives."

B. J. should have turned around right then and gone home. But home was currently a small yellow frame house that didn't belong to her in a town where her only friend was a sister who didn't understand that lawyers don't have time to mend broken hearts.

According to Stephen, B. J. didn't even have a heart. Maybe he was right.

Sighing, she upended the box and shook its contents onto the ground. Dozens of screws and random lengths of metal clanged to the ground. Hard on their heels was a mass of canvas that the clerk had assured her "any idiot" could transform into a tent.

"My home away from home," B. J. muttered as she sank to the ground and pawed through the mess for an instruction sheet.

The Smokies rose around her like blue-hooded giants, and as far as she could see there was nothing but sky and trees. She guessed mountain goats considered it beautiful, and she might even come to enjoy the view herself if she lived long enough. Right now that was doubtful. The mosquitoes were determined to eat her alive.

She got the bug spray from the trunk and fogged her campsite. It was like pouring a teacup of water into the ocean. A mountain breeze promptly carried her spray southward toward Tupelo, which was where she would head if she had a lick of sense.

She could face down the toughest opponents in the courtroom, but when it came to her baby sister she was a coward.

"This is a two-week retreat and don't you dare come back a day earlier," Maxie had said. "I'll have your office completely redone when you get back, and you can plunge into work."

"No black lights and purple fringe, Maxie. Promise me."

"I promise on the lights, but purple fringe . . . hmmm, that has possibilities." Spoken like Magic Maxie, the interior designer who promised pizzazz.

"Don't you dare."

Her threats were meaningless, of course. Maxie would do whatever she wanted; she always had.

"Go on." Maxie had practically pushed her out the door. "And don't come home till you find a cowboy to ride."

"That's Montana."

"You're a beautiful, sexy woman, B. J. You never know when something will pop out of those woods to eat you."

So far nothing but the mosquitoes were interested. Not that B. J. believed a word her sister had said. If she was so sexy, why had Stephen dumped her like yesterday's meat loaf?

She attacked her tent with renewed vigor. Every time she got it upright, it collapsed. Her only compensation was that nobody was there to see. She'd requested and received a campsite far away from the main cabin. Birds and mosquitoes she could deal with. It was people she couldn't handle right now.

She tackled the canvas once more, and bit by bit it turned into something that resembled a tent. Triumphant, B. J. opened the front flap and crawled in to check the view from the inside.

From the distance came a roaring sound. Unless she was mistaken, there was a train going through the valley.

As she turned to survey her mountain home, her leg whacked the center pole, and her house fell down around her ears. The roaring came closer and didn't stop until it was right outside her door.

Peering through the pile of canvas she saw exactly

how mistaken she had been. The roaring had not been a train at all, but a motorcycle, one that now stood three feet from her nose. Astride the leather seat was the man of every cheerleader's dreams, tanned and muscular, windblown and wicked. Tarzan on a Harley.

His blue eyes crinkled with laughter as he looked at her.

"Need any help?" he asked.

Help from the likes of him was the last thing she needed.

"No, thank you. I always wear my tent this way."

"I'm pretty good with my hands."

B. J. considered herself a sterling judge of character, in spite of the fiasco with Stephen Matthews III, and even with the canvas partially obstructing her view she saw all the signs of a playboy—the wheat-colored hair long enough to look wild but not unkempt, the full lower lip curved into a sexy grin, the tank top that showed his broad chest to best advantage, the tight leather pants that left nothing to the imagination.

"I'll just bet you are."

"Hey, I was merely offering a neighborly hand."

"I don't need help from you, Tarzan."

"Up here in the mountains I go by the name of Crash."

"That figures. Anybody with such a big machine could be no less."

"I have a big machine, all right." Crash swung himself off, then leaned hip-slung against his motorcycle. "Want to see?"

So that's what the hunting knife was for. B. J. wished she'd bought one.

"I'm warning you," she said. "Don't come any closer. I have a knife."

Crash threw back his head and roared with laughter.

"A woman with a dirty mind. I like that."

"I do not have a dirty mind."

"I was referring to my big bike. What were you referring to?"

"Your big bike, of course."

She was so hot, she thought she'd faint. She'd never known a man with such sex appeal, nor such rugged good looks. Of course, all that had nothing to do with the sweat that popped out along her brow and beaded her upper lip. Her condition was due to the tent draped over her head, and the fact that she was as out of place in the woods as a toadfrog would have been in a Philadelphia courtroom.

B. J. drew herself up to her full height, an impressive five nine, even in her hiking shoes. She knew how to win by intimidation, and she wasn't about to let the small inconvenience of a tent on her head hamper her.

"I'm going to ask you politely to leave," she said.

"And if I don't?"

"I'll have to get impolite."

Crash reached into his saddlebag and pulled out a pipe, then grinning wickedly he leaned against his Harley and began to tamp in tobacco.

"Of all the gall . . . You can't smoke here." He

winked and kept tamping tobacco. "Where's Smokey the Bear when I need him?"

"The nights do get cool up here, but there are better ways to keep warm than with Smokey the Bear." He grinned. "Want me to show you some?"

"I do not. I want you to leave."

"You don't have to get testy about it."

"I'm not testy. I'm hot."

"I see." Arching a wicked eyebrow upward, he stuck the unlit pipe into his mouth, and there it remained, dangling from his lips like an extension of his sexy self.

"It's not that kind of heat."

"What kind?"

Years of experience in a courtroom had taught her never to make loose statements that would give her opponents an opening, and yet this hunk on heavy metal made her forget even the most elementary rules. She'd lost ground, and the only way she could get it back was to take charge.

"Listen, Tarzan . . ."

Slowly he pulled the pipe from his lips. "The name's Crash, but Tarzan does have a certain charm. Me Tarzan, you Jane. By the way, what is your name?"

"Jane has a certain charm."

"So you do have a sense of humor. I was beginning to wonder."

"It's hard . . ."

"Not yet, but it's getting there."

Her temperature went up ten degrees, but this time she refused to fall for his bait.

". . . to maintain one's sense of humor with ten pounds of canvas pressing against the cranium."

"Great Caesar's balls. You sound like a Philadelphia lawyer."

At last she'd found his Achilles' heel. Casting off the tent she strode boldly toward him.

"That's exactly what I am." Hands on hips, she went in so close, she could see the tiny gold sunburst in his incredible blue eyes. "A criminal defense attorney, and you look like just the kind of man who could use my services. Too bad I don't have my card, or you could take it with you when you leave."

"About those services . . ." He snagged her around the waist and pulled her in hard and fast. She only had time to wonder at his remarkable and swift recovery before his mouth descended on hers. The kiss was long, thorough, and very wet.

B. J. kept telling herself it would be useless to struggle. The plain and simple fact was, she enjoyed every deliciously wicked moment of being held close by a man wearing black leather pants and leaning against a Harley. The aftershock of being a jilted woman. If she ever saw Stephen again, she was going to kill him.

She settled against Crash, wondering just how far he would go and just how far she would let him. He released her so abruptly, she almost reeled.

"I just wanted to see what a Philadelphia lawyer tastes like."

"Damn you." She wiped her mouth with the back of her hand.

Crash slung his leg over the seat and revved his Harley. "They taste pretty good."

"I didn't ask."

"Yeah, but you wanted to know." He revved his big machine once more.

"You insufferable, conceited cretin."

"Spoken like an uptight attorney." His grin took none of the sting from his words. "By the way, I won't need your card. I'm not going far."

The Harley leaped like a stallion as Crash took off.

"Good riddance," she said, though why the mountain suddenly seemed drab was no mystery to her. The Crashes and the Maxies of the world added color, which was nice if you were in the mood for flaming red, hot pink, and passionate purple, but what B. J. needed was a good dose of soothing blue.

She glanced upward at the sky, a sweep of blue that went on forever. Maybe Maxie had been right; maybe she did need this retreat. Away from civilization, away from litigation, away from the noise of big cities and the strife of big ambitions.

Speaking of noise, the varooming of the Harley had ceased, and in its place was the chirping of crickets, the call of birds, and the sound of whistling.

Whistling?

B. J. whirled toward the sound, and there was Crash, as big as you please, setting up camp not twenty feet from her.

"Just what do you think you're doing?" she said.

"Pitching a tent. Want to come over and see how it's done?"

"You can't do that. This is my campsite."

"And this is mine."

"It can't be. I requested a remote site away from everybody."

"Everybody except me. This has been my campsite for the last ten years. I didn't expect to have a neighbor. Especially a Philadelphia lawyer, but heck, I'm easy. I can get used to anything." He winked. "How about you?"

"I don't have to get used to you. I plan to ignore you."

"That's going to make it a mighty long two weeks."

"You worry about your two weeks and I'll worry about mine."

"I never worry. It cuts down on the sex drive."

Having delivered that gem of wisdom, Crash stretched full length on the grass in front of his tent, crossed his arms above his head, and tipped his face up to the sun.

B. J. whirled around and started packing up her tent. She had no intention of spending the next two weeks in the company of a man whose leather pants were tighter than her skin. She huffed toward her car, expecting any minute to hear a scathing remark from her neighbor. But Crash was as silent as the mountains that surrounded them.

Then she heard it, the sound of snoring. The man who never worried had goaded her and teased her, outraged her and kissed her, then had stretched out in a patch of sunlight and gone fast asleep. And what was she doing? Once more playing the coward. Turning tail to run.

B. J. Corban, the criminal defense attorney known for standing her ground, renowned for winning, revered for never conceding defeat was quitting the battleground after the opening salvo.

Setting her jaw, she untangled her tent and began the arduous task of putting it back together. She wasn't about to be intimidated by the likes of a man called Crash.

TWO

Crash was hungry when he woke up. He had found that catnaps improved his outlook on life, and sleep always called for food and sex, sometimes in that order, sometimes not, depending on the circumstances.

Yawning and stretching, he glanced across the way at his neighbor. Now there was an interesting set of circumstances: a remote campsite, a hungry man, and a desirable woman. On the surface, she was exactly the kind of woman who appealed to him—long legs, lush lips, and a ripe body. There was only one small problem: She was armed with a rapier mind, a prejudice against playboys, and a law degree. Armed and dangerous.

The irony would appeal to his brother. He could just hear what Joseph would have to say when Crash got home.

"You mean you were forced to spend two weeks in the company of a woman with a brain? A *lawyer?*

That's rich." Joseph's laugh was as resonant as the voice he used to great effect in the courtroom. And he would laugh his head off at Crash's predicament.

The next thing he would say would be something along the lines of "Did it ever once make you think what you might be missing?" It was a variation on his "a mind is a terrible thing to waste" theme.

How anybody could consider a lifetime spent enjoying the finer things in life a waste was a mystery to Crash. To him waste was burying yourself alive in briefs and books that weighed more than a bowling ball. Waste was missing sunrises and sunsets. Waste was take-out food in a crowded law office instead of leisurely meals in a fine restaurant or in the backyard over a grill. Waste was workouts at a health club after dark instead of hiking up mountains when the first flowers of spring were in bloom or swimming in a lake with the sun on your back. Waste was putting mileage on a steady sedan, meeting appointments instead of lapping up the miles on a Harley going new places, seeing new sights, and meeting new people.

Present company excepted, of course.

Crash glanced over at his neighbor. She was surrounded by enough paraphernalia to outfit an army— backpacks, lanterns, a complete set of camp cookware, a camp stool, a portable grill, an ice chest, a new sleeping bag still in the original wrapper, and enough guidebooks to stock a small bookstore. She gave new meaning to the word overprepared.

And yet he couldn't fault her. Obviously a novice

camper, she had done what most of the uninitiated do: get away from civilization but take it all with them.

Her tent was now upright, though it looked as if a small breeze would topple it, and she was studying an instruction book for the small Coleman stove at her feet. Crash knew better than to offer his advice. Anyhow, the last thing on his mind was spending the evening in the company of a woman who used million-dollar words like *cranium* when a ten-cent word like *head* would do.

Whistling, he gathered a few twigs, lit his fire, and roasted six hot dogs. A few feet away, his stuffy neighbor made a big to-do of fanning smoke.

"Do you mind?" she said.

He deliberately filled his mouth with hot dog before answering. "What?"

"Who taught you manners? Godzilla?"

"My mother might take exception to that remark, but being the kindhearted, generous-spirited man that I am, I'm going to ignore it."

Crash poked his fire and sent another waft of smoke her way. If he smoked her out, maybe she'd leave. Then he could have the mountain all to himself. A pity, though. And such a waste. Her mouth had tasted like cream and berries. He wondered what the rest of her would taste like.

"You're doing that deliberately," she said.

"Doing what deliberately?"

"Trying to smoke me out."

Looking straight into her eyes, Crash took a long slow lick of his finger and held it aloft. Her cheeks bloomed like summer roses. It was a very appealing sight, and he'd have told her so except for one small thing: She was not his kind of woman.

"The wind's from the north," he said. "I have no control over nature."

"I'm surprised that you admit such a shortcoming."

"My shortcomings are legend." He raked her with a look designed to melt the ice in her veins. "But then so are my assets."

By the way she fanned herself with her hand, he figured his ploy was working. If he'd known mind games were this much fun, he'd have given them a try long ago.

"I'm sure legions of women have confirmed your inflated opinion of yourself. Rest assured, I have no intention of joining their ranks . . . even if you issue a solid gold invitation."

"I don't issue invitations: I take what I want."

"This is probably a concept beyond your comprehension, *Crash*, but caveman tactics went out of style centuries ago."

"You've just saved me a hot dog."

"If that's what you're calling it . . ."

Crash threw back his head and roared with laughter. He didn't know when he'd had so much fun.

"I was talking about dinner, Philadelphia."

She raked her dark hair off her forehead and glared at him.

"Obviously so was I."

"I was going to invite you over to share a hot dog,

but since you're so hell-bent on being an independent woman, I guess I'll have to eat them all myself."

He ate two more hot dogs while he watched her futile attempts to start her camp stove. In her starched safari outfit she looked like some big name designer's idea of a professional woman trekking in the wilderness. Only her dark hair belied the image. It had come loose from its French twist and sprang around her flushed face in dark ringlets.

Out of the corner of his eye he saw her brush it away from her face as she poured over the instruction sheet. With any other woman he'd have lent a hand, but she had declared herself self-sufficient so why not let her sweat?

Not only that, he was going to rub it in.

"Nothing like a roasted wiener on a cool summer evening." He slathered mustard on yet another bun, then bit off a huge chunk. "Hmmm, delicious. Of course, a woman like you probably doesn't eat these things."

"They're full of additives. I wouldn't touch one with a ten-foot pole."

"That's what I thought. By the way, what are you having for dinner?"

"Sautéed fresh vegetables."

"That figures. Rabbit food. Better keep it out of sight, or they'll raid your camp tonight."

She jerked her head around and stared at him, wide-eyed.

"You mean *animals* come into the camp?"

This was getting good. Suppressing his grin, Crash straddled his camp stool.

"There's nothing to worry about. You'll be fast asleep. You'll never even hear them."

"Them? You're still talking about rabbits? Right?"

"Rabbits, raccoons, skunks, bears."

"Bears! As in grizzly?"

"Didn't you read your Smoky Mountains guidebook, Philadelphia?"

"Stop calling me that."

"This is the wrong mountain range for grizzlies. All you're likely to see is a friendly old brown bear or two. They'll be no problem at all for an independent woman with a knife in her pocket."

For a moment she looked as if she were going to hop into her car and hightail it down the mountain, but then she thrust out her chin and squared her shoulders. It was a gesture he could see her making in a courtroom, one that probably struck fear into the hearts of her opponents. All it struck in him was a grudging bit of admiration.

"Obviously the park commission would not allow camping here if there were any threat from the animals. Let me save you a bit of trouble here, Crash. I'm not planning to leave this mountain until my two weeks are up, and if that's a problem for you, then I suggest *you* leave."

"Bravo, Philadelphia. That performance deserves a round of applause."

Three red-tailed hawks lifted into the air when he clapped. He would have taken time to appreciate the beauty of their flight if he hadn't been so mesmerized by his irate neighbor. He couldn't take his eyes off her flushed cheeks and bright eyes. She had thrown herself completely into their argument. Would she bring that same passion to her bed?

She turned her back on him and applied herself to the task of lighting her stove. The sun disappeared behind the mountain peaks, leaving a spectacular trail of red and gold. Night creatures began their evening symphony, crickets chirping, tree frogs singing, whippoorwills calling.

The red-and-gold sky faded to a muted pink then a dusky gray. A flashlight cut through the growing darkness, and by its glow Crash watched his neighbor dig into her ice chest and pull out a carrot. She was giving up.

He reached into the coals of his fire where the last hot dog lay warming in its foil wrapper.

"I've got something for you, Philadelphia."

"You have nothing that interests me."

Crash laid the hot dog on top of her ice chest. "In case you get hungry and change your mind."

The look of surprise on her face was his reward. For a moment she was as soft and lovely as any woman he'd ever seen. And he was a sucker for vulnerable women. He almost leaned down and brushed the wispy curls back from her face, a tender gesture that would have been completely lost on her. She saved him the embarrassment.

"I suppose you expect me to pay," she said.

He stepped in so close, their thighs were almost touching, but she held her ground.

A young moon hung low; he could almost reach up and touch it. In the sudden magic of evening, a million stars were flung across the sky so that the mountaintop and everything on it glittered like the inside of a crystal ball.

Crash loved nothing better than evenings just such as these, soft, sensual nights made for loving. Haunted by the remembered taste of berries and cream, he almost bent down to kiss the woman beside him, a woman whose name he didn't even know. Not the kind of just-for-the-heck-of-it kiss he'd given her in the harsh light of afternoon, but the sort of slow dreamy kiss a man gives a woman he plans on carrying to his bed, the sort of kiss that carries the promise of tomorrows.

Softened by the magic of evening, she was dangerously delicious. He almost forgot why he was standing so close.

"Philadelphia . . ."

He cupped her face and tipped it upward. Caught off guard, she didn't move for one heady moment. Then he saw the resolve come into her face, felt the stiffening of her entire body.

"You have about five seconds to take your hands off me."

"Or what?"

"Or I plant a knee on the family jewels."

He grinned. "You got me there. Brawn over brains. It works every time."

He released her, but he didn't step back. Nor did she. Body heat. He loved it. Even if it did come from the enemy.

"By the way, don't you want to know why I touched you?"

"I never belabor the obvious."

"And what is the obvious?"

"I have no intention of spelling it out. But you can rest assured that what happened this afternoon will never happen again. I'm on my guard."

"I hate to spoil your fun, Philadelphia, but I have no intention of kissing you. I just wanted to tell you that the hot dog is yours for the taking. Everything else comes with a price."

He sauntered toward his camp, and when he turned back around she hadn't touched the hot dog.

" 'Night now," he said. "If the animals go on the prowl tonight, you know where to reach me."

"Don't hold your breath."

Crash's campfire was almost out. He put on another stick of wood, then took his harmonica from his backpack and settled down to play the blues. There was silence from across the way. Out of the corner of his eye he saw Philadelphia lounging in her camp chair, the picture of a woman enjoying the music. Heck, he'd figured her for the highbrow type.

Still, he wasn't going to let anybody spoil his fun. One of the greatest pleasures he knew was sitting in the moonlight, making mournful music. He played a jazz riff that sent chills down his spine. The harmonica was an instrument with passion and soul, much like a good woman, and Crash played both of them with equal skill.

He played through his Harold Arlen repertoire and had started on his Gershwin tunes when he caught movement out of the corner of his eye. Tipping his head slightly to the left he saw Philadelphia's hand snake out and snatch the hot dog.

Crash grinned. "A hungry woman will eat almost anything," he said.

"Don't you wish," she said.

And with that parting shot she went inside her tent. He watched for the glow of her flashlight, but she was too smart to turn it on. He could picture her over there undressing in the dark, inconveniencing herself all because of him.

"Lord deliver me from a stubborn woman."

Crash put his harmonica away, stripped under the light of the moon, then climbed into his sleeping bag. If it rained he'd drag the bag inside his tent, but he didn't plan to miss a single opportunity to sleep naked under the stars.

B. J.'s tent had windows, and she just happened to be watching when Crash shed every stitch of his clothes and paraded his assets around. Obviously for her benefit.

She had to give the devil his due, though. His assets were abundant. No wonder he had legions of admirers.

She kicked viciously at the blanket she'd managed to get into a tangle inside her sleeping bag. This was just what she needed, to be subjected to two weeks of a man who thought he was God's gift to women.

Tomorrow she was going to get out her journal and list his pros and cons. True, she might have starved to death if he hadn't shared his food, but the hog dog was such a small pro, it wouldn't hold a candle to his cons. Lord, did he have cons. She'd probably need two notebooks just to list them all.

On the other hand, maybe she wouldn't commit anything to paper. She could just hear what Maxie would say.

"Why do you turn everything into a law case? Have you ever considered just taking things as they come? Loosen up, B. J. Have some *fun.*"

She was in the mountains, wasn't she? She was in a lumpy sleeping bag on the hard ground with wild animals prowling outside her tent. But would that be enough fun to suit Maxie? Not by a long shot. Her sister expected B. J. to return home with tales of conquest.

"Riding cowboys, indeed," B. J. muttered.

The next thing she knew Crash would don a cowboy hat. Not that it would have the least bit of impact on her. No, indeedy. Not even if he hung it on his sizable asset.

THREE

When she first came awake B. J. wasn't certain whether she'd heard something or whether she was dreaming. Tense, she lay in her bag with her eyes wide open, adjusting to the darkness. The wind whispered through the pines, and from somewhere deep in the forest an owl screeched his mournful question.

"Great," she said. "Just what I need."

Tires swishing against wet pavement and sirens in the distance were music to her ears, but after two weeks of woodland symphonies she would go home bleary-eyed and befuddled from lack of sleep.

B. J. closed her eyes and settled into her bag to wait out the rest of the night. She was just drifting off when something jarred her awake. Definitely a sound. She cocked her ears. There it was again. A scratching sound. Right outside her tent.

She rammed her fist into her mouth to stifle a

scream. The scratching came again, and backlit by the moon, a giant claw cast a shadow on her tent.

B. J. leaped out of her bag and kicked it out of her way. The thought of sharing her quarters with a bear propelled her out of the tent, screaming.

She raced outside, looking neither right nor left. The mere idea of a bear was enough to give her heart failure: She had no intention of looking for the actual animal. Her mad dash for safety carried her up the rise toward the form stretched out in his sleeping bag.

She stumbled in the dark and fell with a whump, straight into the arms of Crash.

"Whoa, there. Where're you going in such a hurry?"

"A bear . . ."

Incoherent with fear, she hid her face in the first available spot. It never even registered that she was cowering against Crash's broad shoulder.

"A bear? Where?"

"Over there . . ." She gestured wildly. "By my tent. Trying to get in."

"I don't blame him."

A pair of strong arms tightened around her, and her world righted. For the first time in months she felt safe. For the first time since she'd stood at the back of the church and heard Stephen's fatal announcement, she felt a sense of order in her world. She felt the ground beneath her feet, knew the boundaries, understood the limits . . . and glimpsed the possibilities.

"There, there," Crash whispered, his breath warm

on her skin. "Hush now. I'm here. Everything is going to be all right. I'm here."

It was so simple: She needed him and Crash was there. Forget the pros and cons. Forget her history and his reputation. Forget that they had absolutely nothing in common. Forget that they wouldn't look twice at each other in a different place, a different set of circumstances.

For once she was going to heed Maxie's advice and take things as they were. She allowed herself the luxury of fear; she allowed herself the luxury of cowering; she allowed herself the luxury of messy emotions.

"He had huge claws and he was scratching and I thought he was going to come inside and attack."

"Nothing is going to attack you."

"Promise?"

"I promise."

Sniffling, she buried her face deeper. His chest was wide and solid, sprinkled with hair that tickled her nose and her lips. He smelled like the great outdoors, fresh and clean and invigorating. She reveled in his unabashed nakedness, his brute strength, his superb masculinity. She'd never known a man so blatantly *male*.

She actually wallowed against him. Maxie would have approved.

"It's not that I'm a coward," she said.

"Not at all."

"I'm a city girl. In Philadelphia bears don't roam the streets and scratch on walls and threaten women who never wanted to come to the woods in the first place."

"You didn't want to come?"

He caressed her back with slow, sensual movements. The logical part of her brain knew that a man like Crash would seize every opportunity to turn circumstances to his advantage. But at the moment, she didn't care. He was using her and she was using him. It seemed a fair exchange.

Besides, she still needed his strong shoulder. She hadn't let herself need in a long time, and it felt good.

"My sister said the change would do me good, but what will that matter if I get eaten by a wild animal?"

"You're in no danger from wild animals."

She wasn't so sure about that. Crash was the wildest animal she knew, and she could smell danger all over him.

"Except you," she said.

He chuckled. "Not even me, Philadelphia."

His remark touched a raw nerve, and she shoved away from his chest. "You think I'm unattractive."

"I didn't say that. You're a very beautiful woman."

"You think I'm not sexy."

"On the contrary: You're extraordinarily sexy."

"That I don't have a heart."

"I know nothing about your heart."

All the rage she felt at Stephen boiled over, and she let it spill onto Crash.

"I don't need to be rejected by a backwoods Romeo. Once was enough."

The moonlight turned his hair to a shining halo of silver and his eyes to something that rivaled the stars. But it wasn't his good looks that caught B. J.'s eye, it was the expression on his face. The shallow man she thought she knew became somebody else, somebody with intelligence and compassion and sensitivity stamped all over him.

With a tenderness she'd never dreamed possible, he leaned over and brushed her hair back from her forehead, then let his hand slide down her cheek and rest there, warm and reassuring.

"Whoever rejected you was a fool, Philadelphia."

Tears clogged her throat and blurred her vision. She was close to bawling. Wouldn't that be the last straw? What was he going to think of her? Not that it mattered one way or the other, but she certainly didn't want to be perceived as a bimbo in heat. After wallowing all over him, she was in danger of using the ultimate feminine ploy: tears. Worse, she was in danger of spilling her guts.

She jumped up and thrust out her chin. It was what she always did in the courtroom when she went in for the kill.

"If you think I'm going to dissolve into tears and melt into your arms, you're sadly mistaken."

"The thought never entered my mind, Philadelphia."

"Don't underestimate me and don't dare condescend to me."

"Never," he said, sounding as if he meant just the opposite.

This conversation wasn't going at all the way she'd planned. But then, nothing had gone the way she'd planned for months. Why should tonight be any different?

"I don't need you," she said. "I don't need any man."

"I can see you don't." His grin was the most wicked thing she'd ever seen.

"By the way, Philadelphia, you look cute in that nightshirt. Are you wearing anything underneath?"

She whirled around and stormed toward her tent.

"What about the bear?" he called.

She stopped in mid-stride. Crash was the kind of man to avoid at all costs, but given her options, he was her best choice. She retraced her steps and sat down in front of his tent in spite of the fact that he was still lolling in his bag like some kind of primitive god.

"Make yourself right at home," he said.

"Don't mind me. I'm just going to sit here till daylight."

"Be my guest."

Crash threw aside his sleeping bag and paraded around in front of her without a stitch.

"I'm not impressed," she said.

"I'm not trying to impress you, Philadelphia. I'm trying to help you."

For goodness' sake, how? By showing her exactly what she was missing? Not that Stephen was anything to compare with Crash. No indeed. Using the Maxie Method of comparing men to animals, Stephen was a mouse, a selfish little rodent who snatched cheese from other people's plates, while Crash was a prancing, pawing, snorting Brahman bull.

"I don't need that kind of help," she said.

He exploded with laughter.

"What's so funny?"

"You never disappoint me, Philadelphia. Always thinking about sex."

"I guess it's the company I'm forced to keep."

"It could be worse. It could be an animal without manners." Crash grabbed a pair of shorts.

"What are you doing?"

"Disappointed?" His teeth flashed white in the moonlight as he grinned at her.

"Don't flatter yourself. I'm not one of your bimbos who swoon at the sight of your body."

"I see."

He pulled on his boots without socks. Any other man would have looked ridiculous dressed in boxer shorts and boots, but he looked like a pirate roused from sleep and dashing off to battle.

"I'm going to see about a bear. Want to come?"

"Do you think I'm crazy?"

As he strode toward her tent, she pictured him being attacked. And then what would she do?

"Wait." She caught up with him. "Don't go over there. It's dangerous."

"Where did this sudden concern come from?"

"I don't want you to be torn to bits."

"You kind of like me, do you?"

"It has nothing to do with you. I'm selfish. If anything happens to you, I'll be all alone."

"Philadelphia, I have a confession to make."

"Save it for your priest. I'm fresh out of mercy."

"Would you cut the acerbic comments for a minute and listen?"

So, the man had a brain. Not only a brain but maybe a conscience.

"I'm all ears, Crash."

He raked her from head to toe with knowing eyes. "Hardly," he said.

Thank heavens the darkness covered up the hot flush on her cheeks.

"What's this confession of yours?"

"There are no bears at your tent."

"I heard him and saw him."

"You saw him?"

"I saw his claws."

"Philadelphia, if a bear had come to your tent, I'd have known."

"How? You were asleep."

"Dozing a little, but mostly watching your tent to see if I could catch a glimpse of leg. Besides, bears are rarely seen on this side of the mountain."

"You lied to me."

"I just made your trip a little more colorful, that's all."

"I can do without color, thank you very much."

She huffed ahead of him, stomping the ground as hard as she dared, considering her bare feet. Pain shocked the sole of her foot when she rammed a rock, but she bit her lip and kept going.

"Wait up, Philadelphia."

"There's nobody here by that name. Go back to your own camp."

"I've got to see what scared you."

"You said it wasn't a bear. And even if it was, I prefer his company to yours."

"You've got a stinger a mile long. Did you ever think about pulling it in for a change?"

"When I need advice from a lying Tarzan on a Harley, I'll ask."

"I've been called worse."

"I'll just bet you have."

He matched her stride for stride. There was something comforting about having a powerful male beside her in the wilderness in the dark. But she wasn't about to tell him so.

Ahead her tent loomed white in the shadows. *Something* was out there, and she was secretly glad that Crash had come along to identify the intruder. But she wasn't about to tell him that, either.

In fact, starting tomorrow she was going to stay in her camp and let him stay in his. It would be safer that way. She was starting to enjoy their sparring matches, and *enjoyment* was entirely too mild to describe what she'd felt lolling around with him in his sleeping bag. Freedom was a more apt term. And wildness. And hunger.

She might as well admit it. Crash brought out the animal in her, an animal she'd never known existed, an erotic, sensual, passionate she-beast who wanted nothing more than to cavort naked with her mate.

A woman could get used to feeling that way.

"I think I see your intruder," Crash said.

Coming out of her trance, B. J. clutched his arm.

"Where?"

"Over there."

He pointed toward the back of her tent, but she couldn't see a thing.

"Wait here. It's a small animal, probably a coon or a skunk. I know how to creep up on him without scaring him."

"Scaring *him*? What about me?"

"Just think about Kansas, Dorothy, and you'll be all right."

He left her standing by herself in the dark. She guessed there were people in the world who appreciated nature enough to find beauty in situations such as this. She was sleepy and grumpy and her foot was beginning to hurt where she'd stomped on a sharp object, and she hated nature besides. In addition, the moon ducked behind a dark cloud and it started to rain. Not hard, but hard enough to plaster her hair to her head and her nightshirt to her body.

What she should have told Maxie was, "If you're so all-fired set on somebody going to the wilderness, *you* go."

But no, she had to be the good sister, the one who always did what everybody expected of her.

Maybe that's why Stephen had dumped her. Maybe he wanted a woman who would surprise him every now and then. Maybe he wanted a woman who would spit fire every once in a while. Maybe he wanted a woman with an acerbic wit who liked wallowing naked on a sleeping bag.

She'd ask Maxie when she got home. If she ever got

home. At the moment it looked doubtful. First a small animal invaded her camp. Next a bear. Or maybe Crash.

Now there was a thought to take to bed and dream on.

"Look who your visitor turned out to be."

Crash was heading toward her with a small animal cradled in his arms.

"Stay back. I don't care to view wild animals up close."

"This is not a wild animal. It's just a little old stray puppy somebody tossed out on the road."

"A puppy?"

"Smart little fellow. Finding us this deep in the woods."

The puppy in Crash's arms whimpered, and B. J. melted.

"How could anybody do such a thing?"

Ignoring the rain and the darkness and Crash's bemused scrutiny, she rubbed the puppy's damp fur. She almost cried when he licked her hand.

"He likes me," she said.

"Of course he does, Philadelphia. What's not to like?"

Crash placed the puppy in her arms, and she fell in love on the spot. With the small animal, of course, though the large one was more tempting by the minute.

The wonderful thing about loving a puppy was the certainty that he would never leave her for a younger woman.

FOUR

"Poor little thing," she said. "Poor baby."

Oblivious to the rain, she cuddled the wet, whimpering puppy to her chest, stroking and crooning. Crash was caught completely off guard. He hadn't expected that from her; he'd thought she'd be the squeamish type, repulsed by a wet, muddy animal. Instead she was acting like a mother with a frightened child.

Her hair was wet, her nightshirt was damp and wilted looking, and her bare feet were muddy. He'd never seen a woman as appealing. If he wasn't careful, he was going to have to revise his opinion of her.

Even worse, he might have to revise his opinion of himself. In this wilderness retreat with Philadelphia he was acting more like his brother Joseph than himself. Next thing he knew he'd be wanting to know Philadelphia's name, where she came from, her phone number, whether she liked sailing in the summer and skiing in the winter, whether she preferred sun or snow, what kind of cake she liked on her birthday. Things like that. Things that bound a man to a woman.

He wasn't planning to be bound to any woman, particularly not the likes of Philadelphia. Though standing there with that wet nightshirt hugging her lush body, she made keeping his distance hard. Practically impossible.

The puppy was now rooting around her chest, looking for something delicious to latch onto. Crash envied him. He wouldn't mind latching on himself, and he had no doubt that her breasts would be every bit as delicious as her mouth.

"I think he's hungry," she said.

So was he, hungry for more than he cared to admit. He couldn't remember the last time he'd been satisfied by a relationship with a woman. No matter how good the sex was he always went away vaguely disappointed and wondering what he was missing.

"There's no telling how long he'd been wandering around in the woods before he came upon your tent," he said.

He and the puppy had a lot in common. He'd done quite a bit of wandering around himself. The only difference was, he wasn't lost. Unless you believed Joseph.

"When are you going to find yourself?" he was fond of saying. "When are you going to settle down?"

Settling down had all the appeal of having teeth pulled without benefit of novocaine.

Altogether it was best to concentrate on the puppy instead of the woman holding it.

"Let's find the little fellow something to eat," he said.

"Where are you going?" There was real alarm in her voice.

"To my camp to get a hot dog."

"I have food here."

"I don't think he'll go for carrot sticks." He chucked her under the chin, partly to get a rise out of her, but mostly because he couldn't resist touching her. "Relax, Philadelphia. I'll be back so quick, you won't even miss me."

She swatted his hand away. "The first thing I'm going to teach Baxter is how to bite."

"Baxter?"

"That's his name."

"That sounds like somebody's butler. I was thinking of naming him Butch or Hank or Jaws."

"You would. Those are the most ridiculous names I've ever heard of. Thank goodness he came to my tent instead of yours."

"I'm the one who found him."

"Are you claiming custody?"

"This is not a courtroom, Philadelphia. This is the wilderness. Out here it's survival of the fittest; the strong take what they want."

"I was beginning to think of you as less than a brute. Thank you for that reminder, Tarzan."

"Does that crack mean you don't want my hot dog?"

It was still raining and he was ready to go to bed.

Not that it wasn't fun standing around in his underwear ruffling Philadelphia's feathers, but he was beginning to get chilled.

She gave him a look that would wilt rubber trees, then suddenly she burst out laughing.

"What's so funny?" he said.

"You know what I was thinking? That you looked absurd standing in the rain in your underwear, and then I realized I was doing the same thing. Not my underwear, exactly, but my nightshirt."

Absurd? Sexy would have been more to his liking, but the least she could have said was *silly*.

"We're quite a pair, Philadelphia."

"We're not a pair. I'm an attorney on a forced holiday, and you're a playboy on God knows what kind of mission. The only thing we have in common is the puppy."

"At least you admit that he's half mine."

"Go on and get your hot dog, Crash, but please put some clothes on before you come back."

"Tempted, Philadelphia?"

"No matter what you or anybody else thinks, I'm not made of iron."

With that parting shot, she stalked off and went inside her tent, carrying their dog. He would have to demand equal time, or at the very least, visitation rights.

Back at his camp Crash stripped out of his wet shorts and into a pair of dry ones, muttering to himself the whole time.

He jerked a denim shirt out of his canvas bag. "Why didn't I tell her to bring the dog over here if she wants him to eat. I'm the one with the decent food."

He was so flustered that he tried to get his jeans on over his boots. The legs were too tight, and he knew the boots wouldn't go through in a million years, but he kept up the struggle anyhow, just on general principle.

"Son of a gun." He flopped onto the ground and jerked off his boots, then threw them in the corner of his tent. "Caesar on a mountain."

What did he need a dog for, anyhow? Feedings and getting up in the middle of the night to let him outside. Worrying about the neighborhood cat scratching his eyes and anxious trips to the vet.

The next thing you know he'd be looking for a sidecar for the Harley and a dog-sized motorcycle helmet.

"I'll just not go back," he said. "That's the thing. Let her sit over there with her carrots and her highfalutin words. I don't need this garbage."

He stared at his boots and thought about being called absurd.

"Caesar in a goatcart," he muttered. The least he could do was go over there and prove her wrong.

On the way out he grabbed a frayed towel out of his bag. Baxter had to have something to sleep on, didn't he?

B. J. told herself she didn't care whether he came back; she told herself she was putting on her prettiest rose-colored cotton shirt because she was wet and cold.

She'd called him absurd, but she was the absurd one, primping for Crash as if she were a teenager on her first date. Just as she started stripping off her rosy blouse, Baxter jumped against her leg and barked.

She refastened her blouse, then bent to pet him.

"You're right, Baxter. I have to wear something. Besides, he'll be here any minute."

What was keeping him? He'd been gone long enough to change clothes a dozen times. Baxter grabbed the legs of her jeans and tugged, a not-so-subtle reminder that he had more important things to think about than her paranoia.

"Of course he's not coming back. Why should he?"

She sat down and put the puppy in her lap. "Be glad you're a man, Baxter."

Baxter gave her a look that showed more intelligence than some of the clients she'd defended.

"That's right, little fellow. No matter what folks tell you to the contrary, men still make the rules, and if we don't bow and scrape and kowtow, we're out in the cold with somebody half our age sitting in our warm spot."

"Talking to yourself, Philadelphia?"

She'd been so busy talking to Baxter, she hadn't noticed him slip into her tent. But there he was, twice as big as she'd remembered and four times as handsome. In a denim shirt unbuttoned to show off his chest and jeans tight enough to display his assets, he was what Maxie meant when she'd said, "There are some men you'd just like to lick all over. If you see one in the Smokies, don't think; just do it."

B. J. held on to Baxter to keep from following Maxie's advice.

"I didn't hear you come in."

"I'm that kind of guy. I just sneak up on a woman, and before you know it . . ." He snapped his fingers. "Bam. She's hooked. Just like that."

"Are you naturally this obnoxious, or do you have to work at it?"

"All my talents are natural. Want to see some more of them?"

"No. Just put the hot dog down and leave."

"Not a chance."

He reminded her of a panther when he moved, with all the big jungle cat's grace and twice its predatory nature. The tent was small and he was big, but did he have to sit so close? His thighs rammed intimately against hers, and she had nowhere to move.

Forget the electricity that jolted through her, she told herself. Forget that she couldn't breathe. Forget that she wished he'd throw her onto her sleeping bag and have his wicked way with her.

There, she'd admitted it. She didn't want a Stephen who courted her with ginger flowers shipped all the way from Hawaii and with Godiva chocolates in a white satin box tied with gold ribbon. She wanted Tarzan with his Harley-sized equipment. She wanted a bawdy romp that would wipe every derogatory thing Stephen had ever said right out of her mind.

Which just proved Maxie's theory. She needed a break.

"But not that kind," she muttered.

"Did you say something to me?" Crash asked.

"I was talking to Baxter. He's nibbling my legs."

"Now there's a dog who knows a good thing."

She almost forgave Crash all his inflammatory remarks.

"Did you bring something for him to eat?"

"Mission accomplished."

He plucked the puppy from her lap and put it on his own. Then he pulled out a hot dog and fed Baxter, one tiny bite at a time. This could take the rest of the night, and she had no idea how she'd survive such extended close contact with her high moral standards intact.

That is, if she had any moral standards left. She was beginning to have her doubts.

"I can do that," she said. "You don't have to stay."

"And abandon Baxter? Do you want him to grow up feeling unloved?"

He certainly wasn't going to feel unloved the way Crash was pampering him. She'd never thought she would envy a dog. But there she was, sitting in a tent in the wilderness watching a big man's hands gentling a small dog, and she wished her life were that simple: look helpless and have all your needs met.

"He likes it," Crash said, grinning at her.

Who wouldn't? Baxter would probably like dirt with Crash feeding it to him that way, stroking, caressing, praising.

"That's a good boy," he said to the puppy. "Aren't you smart? You know who loves you, don't you, boy? That's a big boy. You know who your pal is."

"Alienation of affection," B. J. said.

"What?"

"After you've finished trying to win him away, he'll never want to stay with me."

"Are you jealous . . . or envious?"

She was furious at herself for being so transparent. "Envious of a dog? You've got to be kidding."

A big grin lit Crash's face, and his eyes sparkled with mischief.

"Actually I was talking about me. I do have great dog-caring abilities, but hey, if you want to envy this poor little old helpless creature some tender loving care, that's fine with me."

"I do *not* envy the dog."

"It kind of makes up for being called absurd," he said.

She was astonished that this man had a vulnerability, let alone that he would admit it. Though she was still raw from being spurned by Stephen, though she had learned some very bad lessons about men the hard way, she was not the kind of woman who took pleasure in hurting men, or anybody else for that matter.

Her tongue was her armor, not a weapon.

She reached out to him, intending merely to touch, to pat his arm or touch his hand or give him some other gesture that could be interpreted in no way except platonic. Instead he turned, she turned, and her hand landed on his cheek as gently as a butterfly. The lantern picked up the gold in his eyes, and they looked like stars.

B. J. caught her breath. Both of them went perfectly still. The connection was tiny—the tips of her fingers against his cheek—and yet she felt it all the way down to her toes.

"Philadelphia . . ."

"You can call me Jane."

She couldn't bring herself to remove her hand from his cheek. Slowly the tip of her tongue flicked out and licked her bottom lip.

"Is that your name?"

"My sister calls me that sometimes. When she wants to really get my attention."

His intense scrutiny made her shiver.

"I really want to get your attention."

His voice was as soft as the rain that pattered against the roof of her tent. She was vaguely aware of movement—of him setting the dog aside, of the way he turned toward her, of his hands on her face.

"I'm sorry," she whispered.

"I'm not."

He shifted toward her, not so much a shifting of body as a shifting of soul. It was a subtle change that shone through his eyes. She knew then that he was going to kiss her, just as she knew that it would be the kind of kiss a woman never forgets, the kind that imprints on the heart as surely as it imprints on the mind.

In that fraction of a second before his lips descended on hers, she had the option of staying or pulling away. Reason told her to back off, but instinct told her to stay. Deep inside, bone deep where the soul dwells, she knew that Crash had something she needed, something she wanted.

And so she waited, waited for the touch of his lips on hers, a touch so gentle, she might have dreamed it. She leaned into the kiss, melting bit by bit. His arms closed around her, and leaning against his chest she felt the rhythm of his heart, as fast and erratic as her own.

The kiss was tender beyond imagining, lush and warm and full of all the things a woman dreams, so tender she almost cried. Outside her tent the rain pattered steadily against canvas, a hypnotic almost ethereal rhythm that blurred time and place. Cradled in Crash's arms she felt cozy and warm and safe, far removed from the trials of everyday living.

Her blood heated up and surged through her like a river of fire. She heard small animal sounds and didn't know whether they came from Baxter or from her. Warning bells sounded, echoes from her past.

Don't let me make a fool of myself, she thought, but she was already beyond reason, completely lost in the magic of the kiss.

Did he feel the magic, experience the passion? She longed to know but would never ask, never in a million years. For once she was going to live for the moment, take what she could get and not worry about public opinion or consequences or tomorrow, least of all tomorrow.

She was hungry, so hungry, and she hoarded the pleasure like a starving refugee who has stumbled upon a banquet. Tupelo was suddenly very far away, and to-morrow might never come.

Crash growled deep in his throat, a sound half disgust, half regret, and the spell was broken. Abruptly he released her, and they stared at each other, silent.

If he spoiled the kiss with a smart remark she would hate him forever. She might even slap his face. She waited, scrutinizing him as closely as she did opposing lawyers in a courtroom.

His face was a perfect blank, telling her nothing. She didn't scuttle off like a scared chicken, but she shifted away from him in a businesslike manner that signaled she was as unchanged by the kiss as he.

All good litigators were good actors, and that small moment was the high point of her acting career. Maxie would be proud of her.

"It's getting late," he said.

"Yes." She faked a yawn. Let him put that in his pipe and smoke it.

"It's about time to turn in."

He glanced at her sleeping bag in the corner. Was he expecting an invitation? That would be a cold day in hell.

"I brought something for Baxter," he added.

"More food? I think he's had enough."

Baxter was curled into a ball next to her sleeping bag, his head resting on her pillow. Crash handed her a frayed blue towel.

"For his bed . . . unless you plan to share yours."

"I don't share my bed," she said.

He lifted one eyebrow, and the look he gave her said the Crash she loved to hate was back in business.

"That figures," he said, grinning. " 'Night, Philadelphia. Sweet dreams."

"My dreams are never sweet; they're all about winning."

He left, chuckling. She picked up the first thing she could find—a pair of rolled-up socks—and threw them at his retreating back. Baxter pressed himself against her legs, whining.

She bent down and stroked his fur.

"At least he let me have the last word," she said.

FIVE

Crash always slept like a rock, especially when he was in the mountains. After a fitful night spent alternating between tossing and turning and peering out into the darkness to see what was happening at Philadelphia's camp, he was grumpier than ten grizzlies. And furious at himself.

"It was just a kiss," he muttered.

Now she had him talking to himself. He got even madder.

He kicked the covers viciously and glared out at the approaching day. It was barely dawn. Nothing would be open yet, but he would ride until he found something, an all-night bar, a mom-and-pop diner, a truck stop, anything just as long as it provided him a refuge from the woman who had invaded his mountain.

Shoot, he might even find another woman. That was the ticket. Somebody to make him forget a certain pair of lips that tasted like berries and cream.

As a matter of fact, he wouldn't leave things to chance; he would actively search. He'd never had any trouble before. There was no reason to expect failure today.

He revved his Harley and flushed a covey of quail enjoying an early morning stroll in the nearby meadow.

What he had meant to do was race off down the mountain without a backward glance. What he did was crane his neck in the direction of her camp. There was not a soul stirring, not even Baxter.

Memories of the previous night washed over him. He'd kissed her the way a man kisses a woman he loves. It had been completely natural, without forethought or planning. Shoot, if he'd thought about it he'd never have done it at all.

Philadelphia was armed and dangerous. Who'd have thought a woman with a mind like a steel trap and a tongue like a bee's stinger could be so appealing? Especially to a man like him.

He glared at her empty camp stool, at the Coleman stove still unused, at the silent tent.

"Who needs a woman like that," he said, then took off toward the rising sun with the wind at his back.

There's no telling how late B. J. would have slept if Baxter hadn't nudged her. His cold, wet nose interrupted her right in the midst of a dream about riding off into the sunset on a Harley. It was one of those dreams so vivid, it seemed real.

"Good grief," she said. "He's got me dreaming of

black leather. Next thing you know it will be whips and chains. I've got to get hold of myself."

Baxter wagged his tail and licked her hand. She laughed. It was great to have somebody who agreed with every word you said. Not only agreed, but thought you were wonderful for saying it.

"I'm glad we're of one accord. Now let's see what I have that might tempt you."

She thought of having breakfast in her tent, but why come to the mountains if you didn't plan to enjoy the mountain air?

"Right, Baxter?"

His tail wagged furiously, and he had the good sense to keep quiet about the *real* reason she was considering breakfast in the tent.

She put on her pretty rose blouse, "because it's already wrinkled and I might as well get some use out of it before laundering," she explained to her dog. "I don't even plan to glance in the direction of his tent. Not even if a grizzly bear passes by."

Baxter followed her outside, and the first thing she did was glance at the adjoining campsite. She tried to help herself, but she just couldn't. This thing Maxie's books called animal magnetism was real. She wished she hadn't pooh-poohed the idea when Maxie had told her. She was paying for her scathing remarks now.

One quick glance, that's all she'd taken. She tried to make herself not look again, but the effort was futile. She didn't take just a quick glance this time; she got out her binoculars and searched the place.

She'd die if he caught her at it. Fortunately, Crash

was nowhere in sight. Or unfortunately, depending on the point of view.

Of course, it was barely daylight, and he might not even be up yet, but his Harley was missing. A sure sign that Crash was not there.

Telling herself the tingle she felt was relief and not regret, she got out an extra bowl for Baxter and then poured some cereal and milk. After breakfast she was going to have to find a store that sold puppy food.

The all-night diner was perched on the edge of the mountain, its blue neon sign proclaiming that they served the best biscuits in the Smokies and real honey right out of the beehive. Crash ordered enough food for two grown men, all the things that were supposed to be bad for him, fried country ham and biscuits dripping with real butter, scrambled eggs with cheese and grits floating in redeye gravy. Joseph would have a stroke.

"I know you're not concerned about such mundane things as weight and heart attacks, but wait till you turn thirty," Joseph had cautioned him for ten years. Then when Crash turned thirty, Joseph's magic number became forty.

Crash had nine more years to find out if his brother was right. Meantime, he planned to enjoy good food, and plenty of it. It was one of the small pleasures of life.

The waitress was another. She was blond and petite and dimpled, with a ready smile and a cute little swing to her walk. His kind of woman.

He flirted with her over coffee, and she flirted back when she brought his ham and eggs. Philadelphia crossed his mind only fleetingly.

Things were looking up.

It occurred to B. J. that she didn't have the first notion where to buy dog food. Furthermore, her only map showed the major highways in Tennessee, not the back roads and byways of this part of the Smokies.

With Baxter riding shotgun, she drove to the main lodge. The road meandered through the wilderness, and for a while she thought she was lost. Then she saw the sign: Camp Adventure.

She slammed on her brakes. "Good grief, if I'd known that was the name of this retreat, I'd never have let Maxie send in my money."

Baxter thumped his tail against the leather seat. "No wonder it attracts the likes of Tarzan and his big machine." She parked her car in front of a concrete block building with a hand-painted sign that said Office.

"The director is probably King Kong," she told Baxter.

Worse. He had the size of that giant primate but not the intelligence. After ten minutes of trying to extract a map and some information from him, B. J. was beginning to wonder how Camp Adventure survived.

And then she found out. King Kong's wife came into the office, her brown hair in a perfect French twist, her denim dress without a wrinkle, and her smile as welcome as a warm heater on a cold day. She patted her husband's arm.

"Honey, thanks for keeping things going for me. You're wanted at the archery range."

"Bye-bye, Betty Boop." He gave her a big kiss on the cheek, then lumbered out the door.

The woman never lost her smile. "He calls me that, but he's a good man, so I don't mind. Now . . ." She took her place behind the desk. "How can I help you?"

"Let's start with a map of the area. . . ."

Her name was Cindy, and she was sweet, cute, and willing. When she'd delivered his check, she slipped her address and phone number to Crash along with a note that said, "My shift ends in half an hour."

So what in the world was he doing in front of the Smoky Mountains Farm and Feed Supply when he could be snuggled up with Cindy?

Buying dog food, that's what. And all because of a certain familiar car in the parking lot, all because of a pair of lips that could sting like a viper one minute and taste like berries and cream the next.

"Great Caesar in a bucket," he muttered. "Looking for excuses to see Philadelphia."

Not that he needed one. There was the dog. Baxter had taken an immediate liking to him. He'd always had a way with dogs. Dogs and women.

Correct that. Every woman except Philadelphia.

"Maddening wench," he muttered as he passed by the checkout counter inside the feed store. The cashier looked at him as if he'd gone crazy. Maybe he had. Maybe that's what happened when you turned thirty and discovered you'd spent every spring for the last ten years in the same place.

He was getting stale. What he ought to do was pack up his gear and head west, maybe as far as Colorado, or maybe southwest, somewhere down in Arizona. He'd never seen the giant saguaro cactus, though he had his doubts that they'd be half as prickly as Philadelphia.

"Shoot," he said. She was in his mind so deep, he couldn't even get a thought around her. What he ought to do was turn around and leave the store.

Instead he walked down aisles with merchandise piled higher than his head—spray paint, insecticide, shovels and rakes and garden hoes. They even had horse collars. He didn't know they made those things anymore.

Crash picked one up and studied it. It was all leather, with polished brass knobs, not the real thing but a clever reproduction. Next he inspected the cast-iron skillets. His grandmother used to make corn bread in one similar. Where the one in his hand was divided into triangular shapes, hers had been divided into sections that looked like little ears of corn.

Those were the good old days, romping on the farm with his brother, climbing the big oak tree in the pasture, and dreaming about faraway places. Maybe that's why he was such a vagabond. Those faraway places still beckoned him.

The skillet was heavy, and he could almost smell his

grandmother's corn bread. A bout of nostalgia attacked Crash, and he bought the skillet.

His grandmother was dead, and his mother, who prided herself on being a city woman, claimed she didn't even have her mother's recipe, but shoot, Crash could learn to make corn bread. He didn't know why he hadn't thought of it before.

"Do you have any cornmeal to go with this skillet?" he asked the boy at the checkout counter.

"You wanting yellow or white?"

"Does the color matter?"

"Some folks like white, but me, I'll take yellow anytime. It makes the prettiest little corn bread pones."

"Where can I find it?"

"Last aisle, just past the dog food."

"Does it come with instructions?"

"Right inside the bag. The man that grinds it has his mill right here in the mountains. It's his great-grandmother's recipe."

"This is my lucky day. Thanks, pal."

Whistling, Crash tucked his skillet under his arm and headed toward the cornmeal.

SIX

She'd know that whistle anywhere. Clutching Baxter in one hand and a shopping cart filled with puppy paraphernalia in the other, B. J. ducked behind a stack of dog food.

"Wouldn't you know he'd find me here?"

For once Baxter didn't have a comment. She peered around the stack of sacks as Crash went whistling down the aisle. There he was as big as brass, looking as if he owned the whole store and half the mountain.

B. J. wanted to hit something. What to do? Stay in hiding and hope he'd leave, or show herself and pretend he didn't exist?

He solved her dilemma by marching down the aisle straight toward her and stopping right in front of the dog food. There was no way she could avoid detection, and pretending he didn't exist was out of the question.

When in doubt, attack. B. J. came out fighting.

"What are you doing here?" she said, stepping out from her hiding place.

"Buying food for Baxter. . . . How are you little fellow?"

He loomed over her like a mountain, and under the guise of scratching the puppy's ears, he put his hands all over her chest. It was deliberate; she knew it.

He was taking up too much air; that's why she couldn't breathe. He gave her one of his wicked grins that told her trouble was coming.

"What are you doing here? Playing hide-and-seek?"

His hands were still all over Baxter . . . and the front of her blouse. If she stepped back, she'd give herself away. She held her ground and endured, though it was definitely a trial by fire. What he was doing made her so hot, she was ready to burst into flames.

Ordinarily she'd have taken issue with his remark, but it was all she could do to maintain her poise, considering what he was doing with his hands. His thumb was brushing her nipple, and she had absolutely no doubt that it was deliberate.

Besides that, she'd learned long ago never to let an opponent put her on the defensive. Define the debate. Be the attacker. Those were the rules. Rules she'd kept forgetting since she met Crash.

It must be the mountain air.

"Obviously I'm buying supplies for Baxter." She held up the bag of doggie treats. It was then that she noticed the package in his hand, a cast-iron skillet wrapped in brown paper with the handle taped up.

Find the opponent's weak point. Throw him off guard. Rules worth remembering, as well.

"Planning to do some country home cooking . . . or is that a weapon?"

"I'll say this for you, Philadelphia, you're consistent."

"Thank you."

"I'm not sure I meant that as a compliment."

"I'll take it as one, anyhow. Lawyers learn to take all the praise we can get."

"That's true." He laughed.

Something about the way he said it tipped her off. He was not referring to her.

"You sound as if you speak from personal experience," she said.

She was fishing, and he knew it. His old daredevil grin fell into place.

"Great Caesar in a rose garden, Philadelphia. The only thing I know about lawyers is that they're best avoided." His grin widened. "Present company excepted, of course."

"If I weren't such a lady, I'd kick you on the shins."

His laugh boomed around the feed store. Baxter thought it was the grandest thing he'd ever heard. He got into the act by thumping his tail furiously against her chest and barking.

"A lady who loves natural food, big cities, and blues music, and hates hot dogs, bears, and the great outdoors."

It didn't take a brain surgeon to figure all that out, but she was somewhat surprised that he was so good at observation. She might as well admit it; she was flattered, too, though why she should be flattered that a man such as Crash took note of her likes and dislikes was a complete mystery to her.

Maybe something happened to a woman when she got jilted; maybe all her thought processes went amok and her hormones went on the rampage. How else to describe B.J.'s reaction to what had happened the night before. She'd been only a hairbreadth away from engaging in unbridled, mindless sex with a complete stranger.

He wasn't a stranger, exactly, but she knew nothing about his background, his profession, his political preferences. Of course, she'd known all those things about Stephen, and look where that had led her.

There was no way in heaven or on earth she was going to get involved with a man like Crash. Furthermore, she didn't give a flip about his background.

"What do you do for a living?" she said, then gave herself a swift mental kick.

He quirked one eyebrow upward. "As little as possible," he said, then held up the skillet. "I'm planning on making corn bread the way my grandmother used to make it." He raked her from head to toe with a look that sent her temperature up ten degrees. "Baxter's invited over for a bite. You, too, of course, if you're willing to eat my goodies."

"Stop doing that."

"Doing what, Philadelphia?"

"You know good and well what I'm talking about." She pushed past him and started browsing among the different brands of dog food. The one you mixed with water sounded perfect.

"Not that one," Crash said.

"It'll be easier for him to chew."

"It'll get too mushy before he finishes. He won't like it."

"How do you know what he'll prefer?"

"How many dogs have you ever had, Philadelphia?"

"None."

"See. There's your answer."

"Just because you've owned a dog doesn't make you an expert. For all I know your dog is a skinny, timid beast who wouldn't say boo to his shadow."

"Rex is dead now of old age, but in his day he was the king of his neighborhood."

"Which neighborhood?"

"Wherever I happened to be at the time. Interested in me, are you?"

"Not in the least."

She put the puppy chow that needed mixing with water into her cart. Crash added a box of the dry mix.

"For the times he's with me," he said.

"Baxter's not going to spend any time with you. He's my dog."

"Let's ask Baxter about that."

Before she could stop him, Crash had his hands on the puppy again. Under the guise of petting Baxter, he caressed B. J. in a way that melted her bones.

"Does that feel good?" he said.

"No."

"I'm talking to Baxter."

"So was I . . . talking about Baxter."

Crash continued his outrageous shenanigans, and darned if she didn't stand there and let him. Not wanting to make a scene, she told herself.

She began to feel languid and dreamy, and still she didn't back away. Crash was a man without a last name, a man without a home, a man without a profession. Somebody she'd never see again. No one would ever have to know how she'd stood in the feed store in the Smoky Mountains stealing secret pleasures.

When she got back to Tupelo she'd be herself again. No one would ever suspect that underneath her gray business suit was a woman who for a short while had let herself dream about steamy sex on a Harley.

Not even Crash.

He wouldn't have, either, if her body hadn't betrayed her. There was no way she could disguise the hardening of her nipples. A knowing gleam came into his eyes.

"Time to go," she said. "Baxter has to have his walk."

Before he could comment, she stepped behind the shopping cart and wheeled it to the checkout stand. It would be just like him to follow her.

There was a long line at the checkout, carpenters with sacks of nails, farmers with bags of feed, gardeners with seedlings and packets of seed for their spring gardens. The young cashier knew them all and took the time to chat about each purchase.

"I see you're planting Big Boys this year, Mrs.

Clemmons. Good choice. . . . Nice weather for building that hog pen, Mr. Gibens. . . . Missed you at church last Sunday, Mr. Hawkins. How's the missus?"

B. J. glanced over her right shoulder. "Where could he be?" she asked Baxter.

"Looking for somebody?" Crash came up on her left side, grinning. She jumped.

"Quit sneaking around like that."

"I wasn't sneaking. I always come in like gangbusters." He held up a bag of cornmeal. "Yellow," he said, "home ground. Miss me while I was gone?"

He slipped his conversational bomb in just like that, while she was still thinking about the paradox of a man who loved the freedom of a Harley but who clung to the past by making his grandmother's corn bread.

"I'm not even going to dignify that remark with a reply," she said.

He chuckled, and she turned her back on him to stare studiously ahead. The checkout line moved like molasses in January. One of Maxie's favorite sayings.

Good grief. She'd been back in the South only a few weeks, and already she was thinking like Maxie. The next thing you knew she'd be talking like her sister. Which reminded her: Maxie had made her promise to call home.

She finally got her turn at the cashier, and mercifully Crash had been silent, though there was no way she could forget about him. He was like a mountain behind her, a hot, volcanic mountain about to erupt; she felt the heat and sensed the vibrations.

She hurried through the door and had made it all

the way to her car without interruption. If she hadn't been juggling Baxter and loading puppy supplies, she'd have made it out of the parking lot.

Suddenly he was beside her, astride his big Harley, revving his engine like a gangster.

"See you back at camp, Philadelphia."

"Not if I can help it."

"Don't forget, you're invited over for some of my goodies."

The Harley bucked like a stallion, and he was off before she could think of a suitably scathing reply. It took her two minutes to collect herself before she could drive. She stopped at the first pay phone she saw and called Maxie at her interior design shop.

"Magic Maxie's," her sister said.

"I'm going to kill you when I get home."

Maxie's laughter was deep and rich. Hearing it without seeing her, you'd never suspect she looked like a tiny China doll.

"That means the mountain retreat is everything I wanted it to be. Tell me about the hunk."

"What hunk?"

"The hunk that's got you so riled."

"It's raining again, the woods are full of mosquitoes, and I can't get my Coleman stove to work. If I starve to death, it's all your fault."

"What does he look like, B. J.? Tell me you've met a good-looking man who can't wait to get his hot hands on you."

"I don't know why I bothered to call. You've already made up your own version of my vacation."

"Well, all right. If you're going to keep all the good stuff to yourself, at least tell me if the mountains are beautiful this time of year."

"They're beautiful, Maxie. The rhododendron is in bloom, and the dogwood. If it ever stops raining, I'm going to hike into the woods and take a closer look. The downside of spring is always the weather."

"Take pictures of everything, including the good-looking man. You know that only the good ones go to places like that, don't you?"

"What do you mean, the good ones?"

"The real he-man type, the kind who can climb a mountain without getting winded and do the same thing to a woman."

Images of Crash came to B. J.'s mind. Maxie had pegged him perfectly. The only problem was, B. J. was not the kind of mountain he preferred to climb. Not that any of that mattered, of course. He was not her type, either. No indeedy.

"Good grief," she said. "I'm going to hang up now, Maxie."

"Wait . . . Do you like angels dancing on stars or fairies swinging from grapevines?"

"Not in my office! Maxie, tell me you're not talking about my office?"

"No, silly. I'm doing a nursery for Lane and Craig Sutcliff."

"The angels, Maxie. Definitely the angels."

"That's what I thought too. Is the food good at the lodge? The ads said they served real home cooking."

"I don't know. I haven't sampled it yet." And probably wouldn't.

"Glow in the dark or not?" Maxie said.

Sometimes her sister was more obscure than an enemy code.

"If you're talking about condoms, Maxie, the ones that glow in the dark are just for show."

"Condoms!" Maxie hooted with laughter. "I was talking about the stars. . . . There *is* a man in those mountains. I knew it."

"I've got to go now. Bye, Maxie."

"Wait . . . B. J. . . . have fun . . . okay?"

"I'll try, Maxie . . . I really will."

After she'd hung up she patted Baxter's head. "We'll have fun, won't we, boy? Just the two of us."

He made a lively show of agreeing with her, licking her hand, and wagging his tail so hard, his whole body shook.

In spite of her smile, B. J. drove off feeling unaccountably sad.

SEVEN

"Hey, Joe . . . what's up, buddy? It had better be good."

Crash was at the lodge using the pay phone. When he'd got back from the feed store he'd found a note from the camp manager pinned to his tent flap telling him to call his brother.

"You know I wouldn't interrupt your vacation if this weren't important. . . ." His brother could talk about a stumped toe and make it sound important. That was one of the things that accounted for his success.

"What is it? One of your clients has a hangnail?"

"Always joking. Don't you ever worry about anything?"

"Worrying never changed a thing," Crash said.

It was a good philosophy to believe in, but living by it had been hard the previous year when his dad had had a heart attack. At only sixty he should have been thinking about which mountain to climb next instead of which heart specialist to consult.

"What's this all about, Joe? It's not Dad, is it?"

"No, he's fine. So is Mom. Yesterday they rented a Jeep Cherokee and drove through Denali. Snow's still waist high there. Not much wildlife out, but Dad spotted a moose."

Crash chuckled. "He's in hog heaven, then."

Though their father had spent all his life in a law office or behind a judicial bench and only saw wildlife when National Geographic had specials on TV or on occasional outings to places like Wyoming, Montana, and Alaska, he considered himself quite an expert in wildlife photography.

"I'll bet Mom never even saw it."

It was Joseph's turn to laugh. "You know Mom. She had her head in *Women's Wear Daily*. She was making her shopping list for Paris."

"So . . . what's up?"

"I've got a chance to sell that piece of property on West Main."

"Sell it."

"The offer could be better."

"Then don't sell."

"Don't you even want to hear the offer?"

"It's only money, Joe."

"It's half a million. What's wrong with you?"

"Insomnia, but I don't think it's fatal."

"Dammit, Nat. When are you going to quit kidding around?"

Nobody in his family called him Crash except his

great-uncle Nathaniel for whom he was named. Joe said it made him sound like a train wreck about to happen, and though his father didn't say so, Crash knew that he agreed.

"When are you going to start enjoying life, Joe?"

There was a long silence at the other end of the line. Crash didn't bother to fill it with explanations. Joe knew what he was talking about. Four generations of Beauregards had dedicated their lives to the law. They'd labored to bring justice to the masses, leaving their offices and their courtrooms only long enough to see that their wives and children were comfortable. They'd all died in harness, and they'd all died young.

"Look, Joe, do what you want with the property. Sell it or keep it. Either way is fine with me."

There was another telling silence. Crash could see Joe leaning back in his burgundy leather chair taking a long draw on his pipe.

"When will you be back, Nat?"

"Another few days. Maybe longer. Whenever the mood strikes."

"Come by the office when you get back, okay? And be careful on that damned Harley? Will you?"

The only thing Crash was careful about was in not repeating the mistakes of his ancestors. His brother knew that as well as he did, and so Crash just laughed.

"See you, Joe."

When he got back to his camp the sun was high, the temperature had risen, and Crash was hungry.

Whistling, he unwrapped his cast-iron skillet and set about making corn bread. Out of the corner of his eye he glimpsed Philadelphia's car. She must be inside her tent. Probably working. Though he hadn't seen her briefcase, he'd be willing to bet she'd brought it with her.

"Forget about her," he muttered.

He mixed and measured and poured, not exactly according to directions, but according to the way he felt at the moment. "Cooking by the seat of your pants," his grandmother used to say. "It's always the best."

He could tell by the way the batter sizzled when it hit the pan that the bread would be delicious. It smelled good too. He glanced across the way to see if the aroma would bring Philadelphia out of hiding.

There was not a sign of her, nor of Baxter. Where could they be?

And why was Crash wondering? She was cut from the same mold as his Beauregard ancestors, driven to succeed at all costs.

The conversation with Joe played through his head. True, their father was in Alaska enjoying the sights, but he'd done too little of that over the years. He'd spent the best years of his life slaving away for lost people and lost causes, and what did he have to show for it—a pile of money he was almost too fragile to enjoy; a wife who loved him but didn't even know what kind of food he liked because she rarely saw him at mealtimes; and two sons, one a successful clone, the other a defiant rebel.

The law was a profession that ate your heart out, and Crash would be a fool to get involved with a woman born with a brief in her hand and torts in her blood.

He took his skillet off the fire and tested the corn bread with the end of his finger. Perfect. He waved the skillet under his nose and inhaled. Delicious.

There was not a sign of life in Philadelphia's camp. Where was Baxter? You'd think the smell of food would have brought him running.

"Forget it," he told himself as he cut off a big hunk of bread, doggie size.

"Here, boy," he called. "Here, Baxter."

That ought to bring Philadelphia on the run. Madder than a hornet. With the skillet in one hand and the treat in the other, he whistled for the puppy.

Nothing stirred. Not even a leaf.

There was only one explanation. Philadelphia had taken up with somebody else.

"Who gives a heck."

Somebody with a giant brain and a small mouth. Somebody who didn't know Harold Arlen from Herbert Hoover, somebody who thought a Harley was some kind of secret government weapon.

"Great Caesar's harmonica."

Crash stowed his corn bread, then jumped on his Harley and headed for the main lodge. There was always something cooking up there, a game of volleyball or Ping-Pong, a good card game, a lively discussion about the latest bird-watching adventure.

He barely noticed the beauty of the mountains on his hell-bent-for-leather dash to the main lodge. There were crowds of people playing Ping-Pong and shuffleboard, and a large group was engaged in a hotly contested game of volleyball, but Philadelphia was not among them.

He felt like a teenager, cruising for a glimpse of the woman who sent his hormones raging. There was no way he was going to make a fool of himself over her.

"She's the last woman on earth I'd want to get mixed up with," he muttered.

The lodge was up ahead, and he could probably find somebody more to his taste inside at the pool tables or the pinball machines. Determined to put Philadelphia out of his mind, he headed toward the lodge, but at the last minute he made a sharp U-turn and cruised back by the game area to make certain he hadn't missed her.

Even a cursory glance told him she wasn't there. Tall and regal, Philadelphia was the kind of woman who stood out in a crowd.

He raced up to the lodge and parked his Harley out front. If he was going to make a fool of himself, he might as well go all the way.

Philadelphia wouldn't be caught dead in the game room, but he checked it out anyhow, not even trying to disguise the fact that he was looking for her. Next he tried the snack bar and the pool area, though it was far too cold for swimming. The dining room had a few stragglers eating a late lunch, but Philadelphia was not one of them.

There was no way she could have come all the way up there without a car unless the perfect Mr. Uptight and Righteous had brought her.

Crash spotted the camp director's wife.

"Hi, Betty Lynn," he said, leaning against her desk. "How are you?"

"Better now that you've brought a breath of fresh air into this place. We don't see much of you up here, Crash. How're you doing? Everything all right up there at your campsite?"

"Great to both questions. I could take on six grizzlies just for the fun of it."

"Lord . . . why don't you bottle that attitude and sell it. We'd all be better off and you'd be rich."

They had a good laugh. "I'm looking for a woman, Betty Lynn."

"That's a switch. They're usually looking for you."

"I don't know her name, but she stands out in this crowd like Queen Victoria at a convention of chimney sweeps." He described Philadelphia, right down to the tiny heart-shaped mole at the side of her mouth.

"Saw her this morning," Betty said. "She was looking for maps."

"Did she say where she was going?"

"She had a little dog with her, said something about getting dog food."

"Did she ask about anything else?" He tried to think of all the things that would interest Philadelphia. "Restaurants, antique shops, museums?"

"Lord, Crash, you sound like a lawyer." Betty laughed. "That's all I know."

He'd made a bigger fool of himself than he imagined. Philadelphia was not only with somebody else, she was off at some secret hideaway, her lush body spread across a cheap bedspread while Mr. Big Time Score explored all those delightful places that had cost Crash a good night's sleep. Obviously the man didn't deserve a woman like Philadelphia, otherwise he would never have taken her to a cheap motel on their first date.

When Crash was in a bad mood, he always tried to outrun his troubles on the Harley. He'd been to the Smokies so many times, he knew all the mountain trails by heart. Sometimes he thought he could drive them with his eyes shut.

He took the trail that led past a favorite hangout of bird-watchers hoping for a rare sighting of the American bald eagle. A few of them perched on the rocky outcroppings with their binoculars trained to the sky, but there was no sign of the magnificent bird that never failed to thrill those lucky enough to spot him.

Crash stopped long enough to stand on the cliff and scan the skies, then hunger pangs drove him to the nearest general store. Thinking of the good hot corn bread he'd left behind, he picked up cheese and crackers and a good supply of Mountain Dew, then headed into the deep green heart of the mountains.

The woods exploded around her in a dozen shades of green. Spring fresh and dripping with raindrops that sparkled when the sun caught them, the trees were almost worth B. J.'s hike into the mountains.

Almost. Her feet hurt, her left leg cramped, her sweater was torn, and she was hungry. Who'd have thought it would take all day to get to Rainbow Gulch? And why had she come in the first place?

"To see a rainbow," she muttered to Baxter.

Any fool knew you didn't see rainbows every time it rained.

Maxie had brainwashed her. If she stayed in her house much longer, B. J. was going to end up just like her sister.

The sun turned deep orange and dropped over the edge of the mountain, leaving behind a patch of sky as red as a rosebud. She'd seen sunsets, but never one as spectacular. In the mountains she seemed closer to the sky, almost as if she could reach up and touch it. Shivers ran through her. If she weren't careful, she might start enjoying nature.

The sun dropped from sight and a chill descended over the mountain. B. J. pulled a windbreaker from her backpack.

"Always be prepared." She ruffled Baxter's fur, then picked him up and started back down the trail. "Aren't you glad you have such a smart mistress?"

At the bottom of the incline, the trail forked in three directions. B. J. dropped to a log and pulled her map out of the backpack. With her finger she traced her path to the camp.

"Good grief, I didn't know we'd come so far." Baxter didn't seem worried. At the sound of her voice he thumped his tail and licked her hand. No matter what she said or did, she pleased Baxter.

It was a pity all the male population couldn't be like him.

She glanced up from her map at the trails. They all looked alike.

"It's the one on the left," she told her puppy, not at all sure.

She knew nothing about nature, and even less about hiking. What if she were wrong? Nobody knew she'd gone hiking. Nobody would miss her. Nobody cared.

Except Maxie, of course. And B. J. would be food for the vultures before Maxie even knew she was missing.

"I just won't be wrong, that's all."

A big rock shaped like a turtle loomed ahead of her. She'd seen it on her way up. Hadn't she?

Sometimes the darkness dropped so suddenly over the mountain that you didn't know it was evening until you looked up and saw stars. That's what happened to Crash.

One minute he was washing down his cheese and crackers with a Mountain Dew, and the next he was looking up at a sky filled with stars.

Standing on a bare outcropping of rock, Crash absorbed the wonder and the beauty. All of a sudden loneliness soaked his soul, and he caught a glimpse of himself ten years from now, standing in just such a place, his Harley parked nearby, seeing the splendor of nature all by himself.

No one to share. No one to care.

Philadelphia floated across his mind in bits and pieces, the scent of her skin, a wisp of satiny black hair, the curve of hip and thigh. The small empty spot inside him grew until it was the size of the Grand Canyon.

Crash jumped on his Harley and roared down the mountain, trying to outrun his thoughts, but they were waiting for him at his camp, waiting in the form of a silent tent across the way and a car still parked in the exact spot he'd last seen.

The back of his neck prickled. Something was wrong.

He raced to her tent for a look around. The toys she'd bought for Baxter and his dog food were just inside the tent, with just enough food for one meal missing. She'd been gone all day.

Philadelphia loved Baxter. She wouldn't stay gone all day without taking enough to feed him.

Crash had always depended on his instincts, and they were screaming at him now. He ran back to his tent, stopping only long enough to fill a backpack with supplies, then he jumped on his Harley and set off to find Philadelphia.

"We're lost."

The mountains swallowed up B. J.'s voice, and she sat on a fallen log to think what to do. She'd been lost for the last hour, but too stubborn to admit it. The sound of herself saying the words was a painful admission.

B. J. had always prided herself on being capable of handling any situation, but since Stephen had dumped her, she'd felt like an eagle shot from the sky and spinning out of control.

The woods were pitch black, and she sensed predators standing behind trees just waiting for her to make a wrong move. As painful as it was for her to admit failure, she knew she'd made plenty that day, starting with a hike into the mountains without telling anyone. She should at least have stopped by the lodge to tell Betty.

Worrying about what she should have done wasn't going to help her. The thing she had to do was come up with a plan to survive a night in the wilderness.

It was too dark to see. Though she was certain that she'd been walking downhill instead of in circles, still it was foolish to keep going until she could get her bearings. But how was she going to get her bearings, even in daylight?

She was not the pioneer type. She wasn't even the adventurous type. She was a Philadelphia lawyer who had no business in the wilderness.

B. J. wrapped her arms around herself, shivering. She'd gotten her windbreaker out of her backpack two hours ago, and she was still cold. Besides that, she heard a crackling in the bushes. Wolves? Bears? Bigfoot on the prowl?

Tucking Baxter under her arm, she started gathering sticks, venturing only a few feet from her log. Was that a slithering sound in the leaves? Snakes?

That's all she needed, poisonous reptiles slinking around waiting for their chance to sink their fangs into her.

"Go away," she said. "Shoo, scat, get out of here." Baxter thought the whole thing was funny and thumped his tail merrily against her chest.

"If we ever get out of this, I'm going to give you watchdog lessons. Don't you know you're supposed to bare your teeth and act vicious?"

She cleared a spot in front of her log and stuck a match to her pile of twigs.

"Keep your fingers crossed, Baxter."

A dozen attempts and half a box of matches later, she had a small fire going.

Wasn't fire supposed to deter wild animals?

EIGHT

The bad thing about Philadelphia was that she made Crash think too much. A wandering man couldn't afford to ponder. He needed to be on the move, on the money, on the make.

But the really bad thing, the kicker, was that she was somebody every one of his family would approve of. She was like them, driven, hidebound by convention, upright and uptight to a fault.

And the taste of her was so sweet, he couldn't forget her for a moment, not even in his dreams.

He pushed himself, taking hairpin curves at speeds far beyond the limits of safety. There were dozens of trails, hundreds of directions she could have gone.

Not once did he stop to question whether she was lost on the mountain. He knew. It was that simple. The part of the mind that knows extraordinary things told him she was out there somewhere. The trick was to find her.

Off to his right he saw movement. Idling the Harley, Crash shone his flashlight into the trees. A deer bounded away.

He swept the light in a wide arc, searching for any sign of her. In daylight the task would have been difficult; at night it was almost impossible. Still, Crash had to try. Philadelphia was not the kind of woman who knew how to take care of herself in the wilderness.

The trail forked, and Crash swerved to his left, traveling by instinct. He knew this area like the back of his hand. He was nearing Rainbow Gulch, a favorite spot of his. Once he'd seen a rainbow so enormous, the entire sky looked as if a paint box had spilled across it, leaving behind ribbons of red and yellow and orange and blue and green. It was the kind of rainbow that made you believe in a pot of gold at the end.

The hair on the back of Crash's neck prickled. Philadelphia was near. This was just the kind of place she would come to, nature's art gallery.

He parked his Harley and scouted the top of the ridge. That's when he saw it, a tiny bit of blue-and-white wrapper. He picked the paper up and sniffed. Almond Joy. Crash grinned.

So, there was another side to Philadelphia. Any woman who carried Almond Joys on hikes couldn't be all bad. Some folks might argue that the candy bar wrapper could belong to anybody, but he knew better. The minute he touched it, he knew it belonged to Philadelphia.

Jumping on the Harley, he took off down the trail

that snaked to the right. From a distance came a flicker of light.

As he descended, the light became bigger and brighter. It was a campfire. And beside it sat Philadelphia with Baxter on her lap. Caught in the glare of the Harley's lights, she looked like a wide-eyed deer, scared and ready to bolt.

Relief flooded over him, and hard on its heels something so close to joy, he was afraid to examine it. He killed the engine, and for a moment he could do nothing except sit and marvel that he'd found her.

"It's me, Philadelphia." He strode toward her.

"Crash?"

She flung herself at him so hard, he almost lost his balance. Caught between them, Baxter yelped. She set the puppy down, then grabbed Crash around the waist and squeezed.

"I've never been so glad to see anybody in my life."

Crash knew she'd have been glad to see anybody coming to rescue her, but he took it personally anyhow. Now he knew. Underneath he was just like his brother, happy to be somebody's hero, and particularly happy to be Philadelphia's hero.

Wrapping his arms around her, he pulled her close. Never had a woman felt so good. She was soft in the right places and firm where it counted, but more than that, she was exactly right for him.

"Things are out there in the dark." She pressed her face against his chest, shivering. "I saw their hard yellow eyes. I could hear them breathing."

"It's all right, Philadelphia." It seemed natural to

bury his face in her hair and breathe in her scent. "I'm here. Hang on tight."

She made a small mewling sound and curled herself closer. His body responded like an old warhorse to a battle cry. It was heady stuff, being a hero.

"I thought nobody would find me."

The way she said it, sweet and soft and forlorn, was enough to melt even a cold man's heart, and Crash had never been a cold man. He had the kind of heart that didn't take much urging to melt, the kind that could weep over a cardinal with a broken wing. Now his heart was in a warm wet puddle at Philadelphia's feet.

"I'll always find you," he said, and the words came from deep down where only the truth was spoken.

He picked her up and set her on the back of his motorcycle, then tucked Baxter under his arm.

"Wait right here."

"I wouldn't budge if a herd of elephants came toward me."

He started toward the fallen log where she'd waited, and she grabbed his arm, panicked.

"Where are you going?"

"To put out your fire."

He put out her campfire, but when he climbed aboard the Harley and instructed her to hold on tight, he only added fuel to the fire he'd started inside her. Talk was impossible above the noise of the Harley, but that was fine with B. J.

Talk was the last thing on her mind.

She pressed her face into his broad back, and didn't even lie to herself that she was only trying to block the wind. He felt wonderful, and she wanted to get as close to him as possible. Not because he was her rescuer, not because he was the hero of the moment, but because of the way he made her feel—soft, feminine, desirable, and extraordinarily hungry.

So, what was she going to do about it? Six weeks earlier she'd have taken her notebook and listed all the pros and cons. Shoot, she'd have done that a week ago. But there was something about the Smokies, something about Crash, something about being on the back of a Harley that released all her inhibitions. She felt as wild and free as Eve must have felt when she was turned loose in the Garden of Eden.

The roar of the engine drowned out all sound, and the pleasant warmth of Crash's body soaked into her. She pressed her lips against his back. His skin felt hot, even through his shirt. She found a wonderful indentation in his chest right over his heart just made for caressing.

What the heck? Who would ever know?

She circled her hands over that inticing spot, tentatively at first, then with a boldness she'd never have believed possible. The friction of his chest hair against the material almost drove her wild. She'd seen his bare chest, had lolled against it in her panic over the bear. She knew the exact pattern of hair, the exact color, the exact texture.

What she didn't know was the taste. Every fiber in her body longed to know. She longed to bend over him, spread-eagled, and run her tongue around his mouth, down the side of his throat, then into the mat of thick hair on his chest.

She felt sensitized. She could hear the singing of her blood, count the rushing beats of her heart, feel every inch of skin on her body and how it responded to Crash.

Such a name. Full of fun and adventure. A make-believe, devil-may-care name.

B. J. turned her head sideways and looked up at the sky. It was full of stars. She'd never wished on a star, not even when she was young. Always serious and studious, she'd stood in the background while madcap Maxie did the crazy, spontaneous things like wishing on stars.

Was it too late to wish on a star? She pinpointed the brightest one. Venus? That seemed appropriate for what she had on her mind.

Then, feeling a little bit foolish, a little bit romantic, and more than a little reckless, she wished on a star.

NINE

There's only so much temptation a man can resist. With the wind in his face and Philadelphia's arms circling his waist, Crash broke the sound barrier getting back to camp. Great Caesar in a dinghy, what was she doing with her hands? Those little erotic moves she was making nearly drove him wild.

Joseph would love the irony of this situation: The woman Crash was determined to resist had become the very kind he found irresistible: soft, feminine, sweet, and sexy.

What he was going to do was put her down at her camp, see that she was properly calmed down and tucked in, then climb in his own sleeping bag and forget he'd almost been seduced by a female lawyer.

What he did instead was lift her off the Harley and carry her inside her tent with Baxter close at their heels. The puppy immediately snuggled into his bed and went fast to sleep, which was exactly what Crash intended to do. But not yet. Not while he felt the delicious weight of a delectable woman pressing against his body. Not while he was so wound up, he hardly knew his real name.

Moonlight streamed through the small window of the tent and crept around the edges of the tent's flap. In that small and tender light, Philadelphia's eyes shone.

"I don't know how to thank you," she said.

He wasn't made of stone.

"I do," he said, right before he kissed her.

Great Caesar's pajamas, such a kiss. The gods were conspiring against him. There was no man living who could walk away from those lips.

If she'd protested, he might have been able to leave, but as he deepened the kiss her arms stole around him, and she held on as if she'd never let go. It seemed only natural to lower her to the sleeping bag, only natural to fit her hips into his, only natural to run his hands under her blouse and stroke the long, fine length of her back.

She made small animal sounds of pleasure. Any minute now Crash would turn back, but not yet, not while her body heat seared him, not while the flames licked at his own skin, setting him on fire.

He dipped his tongue into her mouth, and she met his thrust with one of her own. The rhythm of tongues and hips drove him almost over the brink. Almost.

"You are so good," she murmured. "So good."

Praise coming from Philadelphia was heady stuff. He had to have more.

He cupped her hips and held them tightly against

his own, and even through their clothes he could feel the hot, moist heat of her. She was lush and willing and ready. His for the taking.

And how he would take her, starting slow and sweet, then building to a wild abandon that would leave them tangled and panting. He hurt with the wanting of her.

Her hand stole between them, and she massaged his rigid flesh through his jeans. Her boldness was as delightful as it was unexpected. He'd always loved boldness in a woman, especially when it was paired with a feminine softness.

His blood caught fire, and he felt the heat on every inch of his skin, heard the roaring in his ears. He yearned for her as he'd never yearned for a woman.

But the thing about Philadelphia was that she was a lady. And the thing about Crash was that, in spite of appearances, he was a gentleman. He'd never taken a woman without thinking about the consequences. He'd never believed in one-night stands, in taking without giving something in return, in casual sex, particularly with a woman like Philadelphia, a woman who deserved so much more, a woman still raw from rejection.

Her breath was hot against his skin, and her heart raced so hard, he could feel its excited rhythm against his own.

"I want you," she said.

"I want you, too, Philadelphia."

It was the absolute truth. He wanted her as he'd never wanted another woman, wanted her with every ounce of his being, wanted her in all the many ways of a man who loves a woman.

He sighed deeply and stroked her back, trying to gentle her down, trying to gentle them both down. His touch had the opposite effect on her. Her hips set up a frantic rhythm as she writhed in his arms.

"You'll probably never know how much I want you," he whispered, the sound of his voice lost in the sounds of wanting she made.

He strained to be free of the constraints of clothes. If she kept up what she was doing, he would soon be out of control. Principles be hanged. There would be no turning back.

"Philadelphia . . ."

Moaning, she buried her face in his neck and raked her hands down his back. Her tongue was warm and wet against his skin.

He tried once more to get her attention. "Philadelphia . . ."

"You taste like sea spray," she said as she pushed aside his shirt to lick and taste along his collarbone.

Great Caesar's stallion. How could a man be noble in a situation like this? Her breasts were lush and firm against his chest, as ripe and firm as honeydew melons. He could almost taste them.

He found the zipper of her pants, heard the soft *snick* as it moved downward.

"Yes," she said. "Oh, yes, Crash."

She had the musky, sexy scent of a woman already wet. He was so close, so close. All he had to do was move his fingers half an inch downward and dip inside that sweet honeypot of hers. He could almost feel her, hot and slick and swollen.

He took deep breaths, trying to rein himself back under control. He was not her kind of man, and she was not his kind of woman. And he wasn't about to make her a one-night stand, or even a two-week fling.

He closed her zipper and shifted his hips back.

"You'd hate me in the morning," he said.

She stiffened as if she'd been slapped. Then she went perfectly still. Better to make her mad for a few minutes, than to give her something she'd regret the rest of her life.

"Tarzan on a Harley and a big-city lawyer . . ." He straightened her clothes, then stood up, chuckling, trying to make a joke of the whole thing. "We're a match made in hell, Philadelphia."

"Get out." She wasn't laughing. She wasn't even smiling.

Too late he realized that she might take his actions as less than noble, that she might even take them as rejection, which was the last thing in the world he wanted her to think.

"Philadelphia . . ."

She picked up a shoe and threw it at him. "Just get out." The shoe zinged past his head and landed with a plop on the ground.

"I didn't mean to stir you up."

She stood up, tall and proud, her head at a haughty angle, her chin tilted upward.

"Don't flatter yourself. You didn't do anything to me. I'm totally unmoved by you, Crash."

That stung. How could she stand there and deny the passion that had sparked between them?

The smart thing to do was leave. But he'd never been known for doing the smart thing. Crash was like a bull, always charging straight ahead. "The most aggravating thing about you, Crash, is that you don't know when to let well enough alone," Joseph was always telling him.

Joe was right about that, instead of leaving while he was halfway ahead, Crash stood his ground.

"Look, Philadelphia, let me explain."

"Put it in a letter, lick it, stamp it, and mail it to yourself. You're the only one interested."

"Did you know that you're cute when you're mad?"

"Cute? Did you say *cute?*"

She picked up a book and threw it at him. As the book whizzed by his head he noticed that it was a volume of LaFave and Scott, *Criminal Law*. That proved his point: He and Philadelphia were totally unsuitable for each other.

"Your aim is improving, Philadelphia."

"Maybe this will hit your fat head."

She heaved another volume in his direction, and he ducked out of the tent laughing.

But he wasn't laughing when he got to his own tent; he was thinking that sometimes the price for nobility was too high.

TEN

Philadelphia was gone.

Crash stood barefoot in the early morning dew, staring at her campsite in disbelief. She'd left, lock, stock, and barrel. There was not a single bit of evidence to show that she'd ever been there. Somehow, she'd stolen away in the middle of the night without his knowledge, probably just before daylight, for that's when he'd finally dropped off to sleep.

"Great Caesar in a hearse," he said softly.

It was all his fault. He should never have kissed her, never have spread her upon her sleeping bag, never have made the first advance toward her.

Suddenly he remembered how vulnerable she'd been the night she thought a bear was after her. He didn't know the circumstances, but he knew that somebody had rejected her.

She probably thought he'd done the same thing. He

could kick himself. Instead he sat on the ground in his shorts and looked into the distance.

If only he could see her again, he'd apologize.

She'd left no clues. Her license plate had said Pennsylvania, but what was she doing camping in Tennessee? Somewhere out there was a woman he'd done wrong, and he didn't even know where to find her to say "I'm sorry."

He didn't know where to find her to say anything at all. Suddenly it hit him: He would probably never see Philadelphia again.

For the first time in his life Crash wondered whether there might be something more to life than traveling wherever whim took him.

"I can't believe you're home," Maxie said.

They were in B. J.'s office, Maxie with hands on hips, her hair tied in a red bandanna, a streak of yellow paint on her nose, and B. J. with her briefcase.

"You weren't supposed to be here until sometime next week."

"Well, I'm here now, and I don't want to hear any more about it." B. J. shoved swatches of cloth and bundles of wallpaper off her desk, then flipped open her briefcase and pulled out her brass nameplate. When she set it on the front of her desk she felt better.

"You mean you're going to work?"

"That's exactly what I plan to do." If she didn't work, she'd go crazy. Probably within the next few minutes.

"I won't be finished with your office till the end of the week."

"Carry on, Maxie. You won't be in my way."

"Yes, but you'll be in my way."

"That's tough."

"B. J., what's got into you?"

"Nothing. I'm working, that's all."

She took a stack of files from her briefcase and spread them across her desk, then she added a couple of legal pads and three pens. Maxie watched her as if she'd lost her mind.

"Why are you doing this, B. J.?"

"I have to earn a living."

Maxie snorted. "You could take five years off and never make a dent in your savings. If I were in your shoes, that's what I'd do." She looked her sister up and down. "Good grief."

"What's the matter now?"

"You're wearing pumps."

"I always wear pumps when I'm working."

"This office is a mess, you don't have a shingle, you don't even have any clients. What exactly happened up there in the mountains?"

The thought of Crash's hands on her actually made B. J. feel faint.

"Nothing happened."

"Yes, it did. I can tell. What was it?"

"Maxie, give it a rest."

"It's Stephen again, isn't it? What'd he do this time? Track you down to ask how to turn on the water in his new house?"

Every room was a stage to Maxie. She swept around making dramatic faces and dramatic gestures. Any other time B. J. would have been amused. Now all she could think about was Crash.

She'd never see him again. She didn't know why that thought saddened her so.

"I ought to find him and kick his aristocratic butt," Maxie said.

"It's not Stephen."

"Aha, I knew it. There *was* somebody in the mountains." Maxie sat on the edge of B. J.'s desk. "Tell me what he did to upset you, and I'll go beat him up."

B. J. surprised herself by laughing. The idea of five-foot-two, hundred-pound Maxie beating up anybody, let alone Crash, was ridiculous.

"What's so funny?" Maxie asked.

"If he knew about that threat, he'd be quivering in his boots."

"Who?"

There was no use continuing to pretend. Maxie wasn't about to let it drop. Anyhow, B. J. needed to confide in her. She and Maxie didn't have anybody except each other; they were not only sisters but also best friends.

"He called himself Crash."

Maxie grinned. "Sounds like my kind of man."

"He was. Wild, unconventional, irreverent. Extremely good-looking and also extremely young."

"How old was he?"

"I don't know. But younger than me."

"How do you know?"

"I could tell."

"Did you ask?"

"For Pete's sake, Maxie. I'm trying to tell you something, and you're hung up on his age."

"I'm not, but I think you are."

"That's absurd."

"Thirty-eight is not old, B. J."

"Tell that to Stephen." Suddenly all the events of the past six months crashed down around B. J., and thirty-eight felt like the beginning of the end.

"Even if I were pregnant right this very minute, I'd be nearly forty before the baby was born," she added.

Maxie pulled a wadded-up tissue from her pocket and handed it to B. J.

"I'm not crying."

"In case you do."

B. J. sniffled into the tissue, then blew her nose.

"It only takes nine months," Maxie said.

"Thirty-nine is nearly forty. And look what happened to us."

Their mother had married late and was thirty-six when B. J. was born. Eight years later she'd died giving birth to Maxie. Their father had spent the rest of his life mourning her death, and if it hadn't been for their paternal grandparents, they'd never have known what it was like to grow up in a family. Fortunately the Corbans had been salt of the earth farming people who had imparted their work ethic to B. J. and their sense of fun to Maxie.

"I'm going to kill him," Maxie said.

"Who?"

"This Crash person." Maxie jumped off the desk and began her dramatic march around the room. "The very idea, getting you pregnant and then abandoning you."

"Wait a minute. He didn't get me pregnant. We didn't even have sex."

"Why not?"

B. J.'s insides jolted as if she'd been shocked. Not because of her, that was for sure. She'd wanted Crash as she'd never wanted another man, not even Stephen, not even the very day she'd stood at the back of the church and imagined them tangled together on the white sands of St. Croix. At night, of course. Hidden by the darkness and a big beach towel.

"Maxie, this is not about sex."

"What's it about, then? I'd like to know."

"Well, if you'd quit jumping to ridiculous conclusions, I'd tell you."

"What's ridiculous about my conclusions? You're a sexy woman in the mountains with a hunk."

"I didn't say he was a hunk."

"You were only doing what comes naturally."

"We didn't *do* anything, I told you."

"Then what's the problem?"

And now they were at the heart of the matter. B. J. felt hot tears pushing against her eyelids. Sometimes she wished she were the kind of woman who could get ranting, raving mad instead of the kind who cried. It was ironic that she was so tough in her professional life and so vulnerable in her personal affairs. You'd think Maxie was the one who would cry at the drop of a hat.

She might look like a China doll, but if you did wrong by Maxie or anybody she cared about, she came out fighting.

B. J. held out her hand, and Maxie plopped another tissue into it.

"That's the problem," B. J. said.

The wonderful thing about their relationship was that B. J. didn't even feel foolish making that admission. No emotion was too messy for Maxie; tears, screams of agony, outright sobbing, maudlin confessions. She embraced them all.

"I wanted Crash and he didn't want me," B. J. added, sniffling, and her sister silently handed her another tissue. "I made a fool of myself, Maxie."

"If I had a dollar for every time I've made a fool of myself, I'd be rich." Maxie grabbed her hat, an outrageous big-brimmed Panama with hot pink and bright orange ribbons streaming down the back, then grabbed her purse. "Come on, B. J."

"I can't go anywhere. I'm a mess and I've got work to do." Even as she spoke she was following her sister out the door. "Where are we going?"

"I know a little place that sells the best homemade chocolate pie this side of heaven. And after we finish with that, we'll share a banana split."

"My hips are widening even at the thought."

"Soul food. It's good for what ails you."

They climbed into Maxie's car, an old blue Volkswagen with stars painted on the top to cover the rusty spots. After a couple of backfires, they drove off down Broadway.

"There's a good movie on at the mall theater," Maxie said. "After lunch let's go to a matinee."

"What's the name of it?"

"Who cares? Tom Cruise is starring. An afternoon of ogling him should drive Bash completely from your mind."

"Crash . . . and I doubt it."

Maxie twisted around to stare at her, and the little Volkswagen careened into a forsythia bush in full bloom. B. J. grabbed the wheel and steered them back on the street.

"Wow," Maxie said. "You really fell hard."

"I did not. I just stumbled a little. That's all. Anyhow, I'll never see him again."

"You never know," Maxie muttered. "Look on the bright side, at least he made you forget Stephen."

That much was true. Not that she had forgotten what Stephen did, not by a long shot, but thinking about him no longer hurt. She no longer fantasized about his new wife leaving him for a younger man and him coming to his senses, then begging B. J. to take him back. Not that she would ever take the scoundrel back, but she would like to see him beg.

Crash was a different story. For one thing, he was not the type to beg. For another, all her fantasies about him were X-rated.

Even now, sitting in Maxie's little car with the air conditioning going full blast, B. J. was so hot thinking about Crash, she had to pull off her jacket.

Or maybe she was having premature hot flashes. Some women started early. Wouldn't that be horrible?

First hot flashes, and boom! she was out of the childbearing stage.

At least she had Baxter.

"We have to go by the house first," she told Maxie.

"Why?"

"I have to check on Baxter."

"I'm confused. I thought his name was Crash."

"Baxter's a dog."

"So is Crash."

They laughed, then B. J. told Maxie how she'd come to have a little mixed-breed puppy named Baxter. The edited version, of course. As much as she loved and trusted Maxie, there were some things that were too private even to tell a sister.

ELEVEN

Joseph Beauregard was one of the most successful attorneys in town, and he looked the part, expensively dressed, perfectly groomed, sitting at a polished mahogany desk flanked by shelves of law books and framed credentials. Underneath the French windows was an antique credenza with fresh flowers on one end and freshly brewed coffee in an heirloom silver urn on the other end.

"Why don't you spiffy this place up?" Crash entered his brother's office without knocking and sat in a maroon leather wing chair.

"Nat . . . I didn't expect you home for another week or so. What brings you back so early? Business, I hope?"

"Hope springs eternal, Joe. No, not business. It was time to leave, that's all."

Joe reached into a stack of neat files on the edge of his desk and pulled out a thick one labeled Properties.

He flipped the folder open and handed his brother a sheaf of papers.

"I sold that piece of property. Take a look and be sure I dotted all the *i*'s and crossed all the *t*'s."

Crash snagged a pen off Joe's desk and signed his name with a flourish.

"You didn't even read it," Joe said, looking aggrieved.

"You guard a penny better than Fort Knox, Joe. I trust you."

"You'll never change."

Crash grinned. "Hey, where's that hope-springs-eternal attitude when I need it?"

Joe left his desk and clapped his brother on the shoulder.

"Glad to have you back, Nat. Things have been dull around here without you."

"I'm duty bound to change that."

"How about a late dinner tonight? I'm picking up Susan at eight."

"Puncturing a few of Miss Perfect's balloons might be fun."

"I'm sure you'll bring the perfect antidote. Who'd you meet in the mountains this time, Miss Dog Patch? Miss Sorghum Molasses?"

Crash had a sudden, vivid image of Philadelphia. Joe would approve of her. The thing that worried Crash most was that he did too. Not only approved, but wanted, desired, lusted after, panted for, remembered. Ah, how he remembered.

Maybe he had been wrong not to pursue her

whereabouts. Betty Lynn wasn't supposed to give out information about her campers, but she'd known Crash for years. She'd have done it for him.

"Nat . . . Anything wrong?"

"No. Why do you ask?"

"You didn't even know I was in the room."

"The best part of me is still in the Smokies." Crash was half joking with his brother, but he knew that he spoke the truth on a much deeper level.

"Are we on for dinner tonight?"

"See you at eight, Joe."

"I'll change the reservations. For four?"

There were at least six women Crash could call, all willing and eager to accept a last-minute invitation. But none of them would be Philadelphia. Not a single one of them could even come close.

"Make it for three, Joe. It'll just be me."

It had been two weeks since B. J. got back from the Smokies, and she finally had her first client. True, her case was nothing at all like the high-profile criminal cases she'd handled in Philadelphia, but nevertheless it was a case that would be tried in court.

Curled up on Maxie's sofa she studied her files. B. J. gave her best to every client, no matter how small the case.

"Are you nervous?" Maxie said.

"This case is not big potatoes, Maxie. It'll be tried in a J.P. court, the lowest echelon of justice."

"I'd be scared to death."

B. J. glanced at her files. "The judge is somebody named Nathaniel Bridge Beauregard. That sounds like some old fossil straight out of a history book. How scared should I be?"

Maxie had a sudden coughing fit then, and B. J. jumped up to get her some water.

Crash parked his Harley and hurried into the court-house.

"What's on the docket, Margaret?" he said as he pulled off his leather jacket.

"Two petty thefts, Wade and Roberts are the attorneys on both cases; one simple assault, Roberts again and B. J. Corban for the defense."

"B. J. Corban? Never heard of him. Know anything about him, Margaret?"

Margaret smiled. "Not he. She. And they say she's supposed to be some big shot from up north."

"There's nothing I love better than putting big shot lawyers in their places."

He grabbed his robe and headed toward the court-room. Margaret made a frantic motion toward his head. Grinning, he pulled off his motorcycle helmet.

"I ought to wear it in there, liven things up a little."

"I don't think you'll need it today. Things are sure to be lively enough."

Crash strode into the courtroom and took his place behind the bench. There was a gasp from somewhere near the front of the room.

He looked out over the small crowd and froze.

There sat Philadelphia, her long legs encased in silk stockings and her elegant neck circled by pearls.

She couldn't have looked more like a Philadelphia lawyer if she'd tried.

Nor could she have looked more delectable. He wanted to snatch her up, put her under his robes, and do all sorts of delicious things with her. Instead he called the court to order.

Philadelphia was obviously B. J. Corban. J for Jane. "Me Tarzan, you Jane," he thought, barely suppressing his grin.

She stood up. He knew that look. She was madder than a hornet.

"Your honor," she said. "Request permission to approach the bench."

He couldn't take his eyes off her. The way she walked in heels was the sexiest thing he'd ever seen. She turned bright pink under his stare.

"B. J. Corban, I presume," he said.

"You have to recuse yourself," she said.

"Why?"

She flushed even deeper. "You know perfectly well why . . . Your Honor."

"Would you care to elaborate?"

She glanced over her shoulder as if she expected a herd of elephants to mow her down at any time.

"Not here," she whispered.

"In chambers," he said.

Their gazes locked, and for a heartbeat they were the only two people in the courtroom. She nodded.

He called a ten-minute recess, then led her to his

private office, vividly aware of every move she made. She didn't speak as they marched down the long hallway, didn't even look at him. Restraint was not his style. He assessed her boldly, enjoying the way she flushed under his gaze.

"Here we are," he said, opening his door with a flourish. "Come on in, Philadelphia."

"My name's not Philadelphia." Inside she moved as far away from him as she could get, then stood behind a wing chair and clutched the back as if it were a lifeboat and she the victim of a shipwreck. "And that's exactly what I mean," she added.

"About what?" He knew perfectly well what she meant, but he loved watching her when her temper got up.

"You can't keep calling me Philadelphia. . . ." She took a deep breath and reined in her temper, but she could do nothing to moderate the hot flush on her cheeks. ". . . Your *Honor*."

"Why not?"

"Good grief." She started to rake her hands through her hair, then seemed to remember she was wearing a French twist. Her hands hung helpless in the air for a moment, then she straightened her collar and adjusted her pearls. "What kind of judge are you?"

"I'm the judge on your case."

She stepped from behind the chair, her hands balled into fists. "You are the most maddening, arrogant . . ."

He grinned at her, and she stepped back behind the chair.

"You can't do that . . . Your Honor," she said, her lips almost white with the effort of control. "You must recuse yourself."

"How's Baxter?" he said.

"Baxter?"

"Our dog."

"I know who Baxter is, and he's not *our* dog, he's my dog."

"How is he?"

"People are out there waiting for you in the courtroom."

"Did you bring his blue towel home? He likes that towel."

"I can't believe this." She threw up her hands and marched to his window. Her neck and shoulders were stiff as she looked out, then she whirled back to him. "You lied to me. I thought you were a motorcycle jock."

"Is that why you were so hot for me?"

"I was not hot for you."

When she lied her eyes got brighter. She'd been hotter than a potbellied stove that night in her tent. Crash hoped she still was. Great Caesar's whiskers, he still wanted her. Now more than ever. It didn't make a bit of sense to him.

"I never lied to you, Philadelphia."

"You acted as if you don't even like lawyers."

"I don't."

"But *you're* a lawyer."

"A man has to make a living some way." Suddenly it seemed important that he tell her the truth. "It's a family thing, Philadelphia. I couldn't let five generations of Beauregards down."

He'd never revealed that much of himself to any other woman, and now he felt vulnerable. It was a new sensation for him, and he quickly covered his feelings with another quip.

"I decided to get in a position where I could do the least amount of work and the least amount of harm."

"Good grief." She paced back to her chair and hung on. "I can't try this case in front of you. Recuse yourself."

"On what grounds?"

She eyed the coffeepot as if she meant to pick it up and throw it at him. He was almost disappointed when she reined her temper under control.

"Why didn't you throw it, Philadelphia? I'm kind of partial to that hellcat I found on the mountain."

"It's because of what happened in the mountains that you should step down from my case."

"What happened in the mountains?"

"You were . . . we were . . ."

She squeezed the back of the chair, and wet her lips with the tip of her tongue. He remembered exactly how that tongue felt thrusting against his own.

"We were *familiar* with each other," she whispered.

Not as familiar as he'd wanted to be. Not as familiar as he wanted to be right this very minute. He stalked across the room, shoved the chair out of his way, and pulled her roughly against his chest. She held herself as stiff as a wooden Indian.

He cupped one hand around her pert bottom and

the other behind her neck as he bent over her. Her lips were every bit as enticing as he remembered, every bit as delicious. In spite of the rigidness of her body, her lips were pliant and willing. He plundered them relentlessly, tasting, sucking, thrusting until he was so hard, he thought he would explode.

When she moaned, he raked her hips close, grinding them against his. Being forbidden gave an exciting edge to what they were doing. No judge would prejudice the case by consorting sexually with the lawyer for the defense.

He knew the rules . . . and he knew just how far to push them.

The courtroom would soon be packed, everybody waiting for the judge. He planned to take full advantage of the few minutes he had left with Philadelphia.

Her body had gone from rigid to slightly resistant to pliant and willing. The soft sounds of desire she made nearly drove him mad. He thrust his hips and tongue with a rhythm that was as urgent as it was reckless. His skin caught fire, and he kissed until they were both panting for breath.

She stiffened suddenly, as if she'd just come to her senses.

"We can't do this . . . ," she said.

"Yes, we can, Philadelphia. That was just a kiss. *Familiar* is when I get in your pants."

Flushed and lovely, she tucked a stray curl into her French twist, then touched a finger to her lips. They looked deliciously bruised and pouty. He wanted to kiss her again . . . and more, ever so much more.

"You should be disbarred," she said.

"Probably."

"You're not going to step down, are you?"

"As much as I'd enjoy the pleasure of doing something with you worth stepping down for, I'm denying your request, Philadelphia. As soon as you're ready, you can present the case."

She glared at him. "I'm *always* ready."

"So you are, Philadelphia. So you are."

She jerked up the glass paperweight on his desk and drew back her arm.

"I do love a feisty woman," he said, chuckling.

She set the paperweight carefully back on the desk, then with elaborate politeness she held out her hand to him.

"Thank you for your time, Judge Beauregard."

He bent and with equally elaborate care, planted a warm kiss in her palm.

"I'll see you in court . . ." Straightening up, he winked at her. ". . . Philadelphia."

She didn't bat an eyelash as she left his office. Watching her, you'd never know she was a woman who had just been kissed. You'd never dream that only minutes earlier she'd been writhing and moaning in his arms.

No wonder she had the reputation of being such a hotshot. If she performed as well in the courtroom as she did in his chambers, she'd mow the competition down.

Great Caesar in a salad, she was a magnificent woman. Even if she was a lawyer.

Crash was in such a state of arousal that he was the one who had to collect himself. He could hardly move in his condition, let alone sit behind the bench and dispense justice.

That was a laugh. Him, dispensing justice. In spite of his general distrust of the system, he still believed that the little man with his penny-ante crimes deserved a fair trial, and he believed he was the man who could give it to him.

Maybe he was the best actor of all. Or maybe he was nothing more than a hypocrite and a fraud.

When he could move, he poured himself a cup of strong black coffee, no cream and sugar. He needed a strong jolt of caffeine to fortify himself to face Philadelphia again.

In the ladies' room, B. J. applied lipstick. Her hands were shaking so, she got it crooked. She fumbled in her purse for a tissue, then angrily wiped it off.

"Good grief, I look more like a court jester than an attorney for the defense."

Her face was still flushed, her lips puffy from Crash's kisses.

"Crash, indeed." Bending over she splashed water on her face. Dripping, she scowled at herself in the mirror. "The Honorable Judge Nathaniel Bridge Beauregard." She saluted. "Sir!"

She glowered at herself some more, then stiffened her spine, tilted her chin, and applied a perfect slash of Chinese red to her lips.

"Nothing's going to stop me from winning this case. Nothing."

Seeing Philadelphia in action, Crash would have thought she was a different woman from the one in his chambers if he didn't know better. She knew her stuff. What was more, she had taken a frivolous case he called "The Rabbit Who Wouldn't Stay Dead" and given it weight and dignity and humor.

Crash didn't know when he'd had as much fun, especially on the bench. Her client, Mildred Perkins, was on the stand, and Philadelphia was leading her through the series of events that resulted in her being sued for emotional distress by her neighbor, Fanny Lou Hankins.

Philadelphia skillfully guided her client through a description of Mildred's dog as being small, old, docile, and afraid to say boo at his shadow—not at all the kind of animal who would willfully attack her neighbor's rabbit—and now she was down to the heart of the case.

"Would you tell the jury in your own words what happened the day you discovered Miss Hankins's rabbit in your yard?" Philadelphia said.

Mildred Perkins fluffed up her recently permed hair, sending a waft of ammonia Crash's way. He could tell by the way she sucked in her stomach and adjusted her glasses that she was going to ramble all over the place. Philadelphia knew that too. Her eyes gleamed with secret triumph as she turned her witness loose.

By the time Mildred Perkins finished with her

story, the jury would be so worn out with information, they wouldn't know the rabbit from the dog.

"Well, it was like this . . ." Mildred blew her breath out between her cheeks and plunged into her story. "I had oatmeal for breakfast, just like I always do right about eight o'clock, right before I let my little dog Tilly out. Fanny Lou goes to work at seven-thirty and I knew good and well she'd already put her rabbit in its pen. But just to make sure, I went out in the yard and checked. . . . I even called him, 'Henry, Henry.' . . . He'd come when he heard his name, you know. Pet rabbits do that."

She paused to gulp from the glass of water at her side. "Seeing that the coast was clear, I let my little Tilly out. Not that she would have done a thing to Henry, anyhow. She was scared of that big ole rabbit. But Fanny Lou was always so nervous when Tilly was in the yard . . . and I didn't want to do anything to upset Fanny Lou. Lordy, we've been friends for fifty years. . . . It plumb breaks my heart. . . ."

Putting a handkerchief over her mouth to stifle back a sob, she looked at her neighbor as if she couldn't believe Fanny Lou would even *think* of such a thing as suing her for emotional distress, let alone actually do it.

It was a perfect touch. Philadelphia couldn't have had better results if she'd coached her client. Crash wondered if she had. Philadelphia was no slouch in the acting department.

Just look at her now, as sleek and shiny and correct as a tin soldier in a display case. You'd never know that underneath that starched exterior beat the heart of a hoyden.

"Go on," she gently prodded her client. The timing was perfect. A small wait gave the jury time to shift their sympathies to Mildred. Too long would have put the focus back on the issue at hand.

"Well . . ." Mildred drew a long breath. ". . . When Tilly commenced to barking I ran outside to see what was wrong. I just couldn't believe my eyes when I saw it, that big old healthy white rabbit all bloody and dirty right there under the apple tree that Fanny Lou helped me plant."

She swiveled toward the jury. "It's right smack dab on the line between our little houses. In the summer me and Fanny Lou pick apples together and make jelly." She turned an aggrieved look on her neighbor.

"And what was your reaction?" Philadelphia gently prodded.

"Lordy, you could have knocked me over with a feather. Poor little Tilly was scared to death, barking and shaking, and I thought to myself, 'Fanny Lou's gonna have a heart attack if she sees that rabbit like this.' . . . I almost did myself. So I got a towel and wrapped that rabbit up and took it upstairs to the bathroom. Tilly was so scared she wouldn't even go into the bathroom with me.

"I like to never got that rabbit cleaned up. It took three shampooings, and then it took me another hour to blow-dry its fur." She looked directly at the jury. "You shoulda seen it when I got through. It was as clean as a whistle. I took it and put it in its cage so it would stay nice and clean till Fanny Lou got home. I even propped it up with a piece of lettuce in its paws so it would look like it passed on natural."

"You were planning to tell your friend Fanny Lou about the rabbit when she got home?" Philadelphia slid the question in smoothly.

"Objection." Ralph Roberts was on his feet. "Counsel is leading the witness."

"Sustained." Crash looked at Philadelphia, but he couldn't be stern to save his soul. "Counsel will rephrase the question."

"Yes, Your Honor." Her cool mask never slipped when she looked at him. He was disappointed.

"What was your intent, Miss Perkins?" she said.

"Lordy, I was going to race out the door the minute I heard Fanny Lou's car drive up and tell her about Henry, but the phone rang—it was Effie Mae, she can talk the horns off a billy goat—and by the time I saw it was after five, Fanny Lou was pounding on my door, fit to be tied, screaming and carrying on like she'd seen a ghost."

Tears the size of golf balls sprang into Mildred's eyes as she stared at the jury. "How was I supposed to know that rabbit had been dead for three days?"

It took the jury only twenty minutes to reach a verdict of not guilty, but Philadelphia didn't wait around for congratulations. As a matter of fact, she slipped out of the courtroom without giving Crash a backward glance.

"A heart of stone, that's what she has," he muttered as he pulled off his robes.

Margaret looked up from her typing. "Who?"

"Female lawyers," he said.

Margaret perked up. She'd been trying to find somebody for her boss for years. She and her friend Maxie had hatched the plan for Crash and B. J. to meet in the mountains. Nature hadn't taken its course. But there was still hope.

"She's got a face and body made by the angels," she said, grinning.

"You cagey old bird. Have you been spying again instead of doing the filing?"

"Spying's more fun. That B. J. Corban's got guts as well as style. Why don't you give her a call, Nat?"

"I don't consort with lawyers."

"Pshaw. You consort with whoever you take a notion to."

He thought about that for a minute. Crash prided himself on being a rebel, on flouting the rules, on being as free as the eagles he sometimes spotted along the Tennessee River.

"If I get any calls this afternoon, you know what to do, Margaret."

"I ought to try my hand at writing a book. Lord knows, you've given me enough practice with fiction." She grinned as he donned his motorcycle helmet. "Where are you headed?"

"To see a dog about a woman."

TWELVE

B. J. called her ad for a secretary into the newspaper, then whistled for Baxter, locked up her office, and set out in search of a house to rent. Over breakfast Maxie had said, "What's the hurry? I have plenty of room." But B. J. didn't see it that way. With the addition of Baxter the little house on Maxwell Street was getting crowded.

B. J. had picked the rental agent out of the yellow pages, and Baxter hated her at first glance. He growled and strained at his leash and generally acted as if Opal P. McIntyle was fair game for stray dogs.

Opal started off being gallant about the whole thing.

"That's a cute mutt," she said, bending down to pet him.

Baxter took exception to being called a mutt and nipped at her snakeskin shoes. Fortunately she stepped back and he missed.

"Are you all right?" B. J. said.

"I paid ninety-five dollars for these shoes." Opal swabbed at them with a lace-edged handkerchief, while Baxter sat on B. J.'s foot glowering at her. "Look at them now, spattered with dog spit."

"I apologize for his behavior," B. J. said, though she was beginning to see Baxter's point of view. "He's generally very well behaved."

Opal straightened up and tucked the handkerchief in her purse. "I can tell you right now, Miss Corban, finding a place for you is going to be hard. Most rentals don't take dogs."

B. J. imagined living in Maxie's house forever, bringing up Baxter while she drifted into gray-haired spinsterhood.

"Don't you have anything?" she said, trying not to sound as desperate as she felt.

"I know of one place. . . ." She raked B. J. up and down, taking in the spit shine on her pumps, the Saks Fifth Avenue suit, the Majorca pearls. "I don't think you'll like it," Opal added.

"Show me."

Opal was right. B. J. hated the place. It was dark and drab and small, not fit for Baxter let alone B. J. She and Baxter consoled themselves with ice cream, then headed back to her offices on Broadway.

Crash's Harley was parked out front, and beside it an old blue Chevrolet with the back bumper wired on.

"Can you believe his gall?" she said, and Baxter thumped his tail.

Her heart was pounding so hard at the thought of

seeing Crash, she had to sit in the car and collect herself. She applied fresh lipstick, then got out of the car and stood on the sidewalk trying to locate the enemy. Where in the world was he?

A breeze stirred the forsythia blooming beside her doorway, a squirrel raced down the oak tree to scold Baxter, and a robin tugged at a worm in the azalea bed. But Crash was nowhere to be found.

"Good riddance."

As she led Baxter to the front porch, she dug for her keys. Before she could fit them in the lock, the door swung open, and there was Crash, bigger than life and twice as exciting. Quite simply, he took her breath away.

Baxter didn't suffer the same malady. He leaped onto Crash's leg, his tail thumping wildly. Crash scooped him up, taking up slack in the leash so that his thigh pressed B. J.'s. She couldn't have moved if wild stallions were stampeding her.

"There's my boy," he said. "How's my big boy?"

Crash petted and pampered and crooned to the little dog, while B. J. stood rooted to the spot, hot all over, suffering from dog envy and possibly premature menopause.

Something was definitely wrong with her. Maybe she ought to see a doctor.

"Yes, that's my fine boy. Have you missed your daddy?"

B. J. felt a jolt like physical pain in her empty womb.

"How did you get in?" she said.

"These antique locks are easy. And the system was a piece of cake."

"You penetrated my security?"

"I can penetrate anything." His eyes danced with devilment.

Her heart pounded so hard, she figured they heard it all the way to city hall.

"Aren't you going to thank me?" he said.

"Why should I thank you?"

"You had clients waiting in their car." He nodded toward the old Chevrolet. "If I hadn't come along to invite them in, they might have gone to somebody else." He winked. "A lavish display of affection might be appropriate."

"I ought to have you arrested."

She pushed past him, forgetting that they were still joined by Baxter's leash. She was jerked back against him with a thump. He snaked an arm around her waist.

"Steady there," he said.

His hot breath ignited the skin along the side of her neck and everything else she had that was combustible.

It was unfair to put so much temptation in the way of a jilted woman.

"Unhand my dog and get off my porch," she said.

"One out of two is not bad." Grinning, he handed over Baxter, then held open the door. "After you, Philadelphia."

She couldn't afford to make a scene in front of clients. That's what she told herself as she walked into her own office on the arm of Nathaniel Bridge Beauregard, the naughtiest judge in town.

B. J. could hardly concentrate on what her client was saying for wondering what was going on in the waiting room. Squeals of laughter came from that direction, followed by Baxter's excited barking and Crash's big, booming mirth.

"Excuse me, Mrs. Parker . . ." B. J. turned a page on her yellow legal pad and poised her pen above the paper. "Would you repeat that, please?"

She hoped Mrs. Parker would think she was being thorough instead of inattentive.

"This rabbit's not really mine. See? He's a wild one that I nursed back to health when he limped into my yard all mangled up."

Jo Nell Parker made every statement sound as if it were a question.

"Let me get this straight. Your neighbor is suing you because a wild rabbit raided her garden?"

"Yes. And when I heard what you did with Mildred's case, naturally I came to you."

B. J. suppressed a sigh. In Philadelphia she'd defended accused criminals; in Tupelo it was accused rabbits. Thank goodness Stephen would never know.

She studied her new client. Jo Nell Parker was a plain woman wearing a faded print dress, a sweater too small, and men's work brogans with white athletic socks; she was an honest, hard-working woman looking to the courts for justice.

Suddenly B. J. was ashamed of her self-serving thoughts. What she should do is call Stephen to say that she was finally doing something that counted: representing the underdog.

"And you don't own the rabbit?" B. J. said.

"No, ma'am. I sure don't. I turned it back to the wild."

"Did it have any special markings to distinguish it from any other rabbit in the wild, Mrs. Parker?"

"Not a thing. It's just an ordinary brown rabbit with a white tail, see?" Mrs. Parker twisted her hands together.

B. J. came around the desk and put her arms around the woman's shoulders.

"You go on home and don't worry about a thing. This case is a piece of cake."

"I don't have much money, Miss Corban, but I've got a garden that'll soon be full of vegetables."

"Are you going to have any cucumbers?"

"Yep." Jo Nell Parker was grinning from ear to ear. "There's nothing I like better."

With her arm still around Mrs. Parker's shoulders, B. J. walked toward her waiting room and the sounds of merriment.

Crash was in the middle of the floor with the youngest Parker boy on his back and two others climbing over his knees. Baxter was untying his shoelaces while the two little Parker girls danced around him chanting. "Ring around the roses, pocket full of posies."

He grinned up at them. "You're not fixing to take my buddies, are you?"

Mrs. Parker scooped her youngest off his back.

"Scooter, get off his back. Lordy, they're a handful."

"Just lively, that's all," Crash said.

"I can't thank you enough for keeping them occupied while I talked with Lawyer Corban."

"My pleasure." He stood up and shook her hand, then swung the two little girls to his shoulders and escorted them all to their raggedy old car.

B. J. figured the best thing to do was lock the door behind him. Instead she went to the window and watched while he bent down to accept each child's sticky kiss.

Her heart ached. She'd never even seen Stephen speak to a child, let alone get close enough to allow one to dirty his cheek.

She was dangerously close to liking this man she'd been determined to hate. When he came whistling back up the sidewalk, she chastised herself for being a liar.

Her toes curled under as he walked back through the door. *Like* was far too mild for what she felt.

When he started back up the sidewalk, she left the window, sat at the receptionist's desk, and pretended to be marking dates on a calendar.

"That was a mighty fine thing you did, Philadelphia."

Leaning against her door, he was something straight out of an old Western, the gunslinger who bursts into the saloon to clear out the bad guys, then sweep upstairs to the bedroom to get his reward with the town's floozy. B. J. licked her bottom lip.

Once she'd played a floozy, way back in high school when she'd put her dramatic skills to use on the stage. Now she saved them all for the courtroom . . . or for occasions like this when she wanted to be the floozy who dishes out the reward but didn't want Crash to know what she was thinking.

"Thank you for baby-sitting." She drew hearts around the edges of May, then a cupid hovering over the fifteenth.

"I like kids."

Crash plucked the calendar from her hands and studied her artwork. She was going to kill him if he laughed. Or even if he smiled. He didn't do either, and she received a temporary reprieve from being the kind of person she'd spent most of her life defending.

Instead he sat in a chair almost like a gentleman with Baxter curled up at his feet.

"I don't know of another lawyer in Tupelo who would take cucumbers for payment," he said.

"She told you."

"I had to restrain her to keep her from rushing back in here and kissing your feet."

Crash studied B. J. as if she were a brand of exotic fruit he'd found growing on his tomato vine.

"You keep surprising me, Philadelphia."

"Why does that surprise you?"

"I thought I had you pegged."

"Never underestimate your opponent. Any litigator worth his salt knows that."

"You haven't been in town long enough. Ask anybody on the street. I'm the only Beauregard living not worth his salt."

He was totally without remorse or self-pity. Nor

was he bragging. Crash was merely presenting himself in the framework of hometown opinion.

B. J. clasped her hands together under the desk so she wouldn't do something revealing, such as caressing her bottom lip or fiddling with the top button of her blouse.

"Is that how you see yourself," he added, softly. "As my opponent?"

Where was her barbed wit when she needed it?

"Sometimes," she said.

"Is this one of those times?"

She licked her bottom lip. "No."

He watched the tip of her tongue as intently as a cat studying a mouse's hole. Too late, she realized what she had done.

"I'm glad," he said.

She realized then the power of words to melt a heart.

But a melted heart was a vulnerable one, and so she reminded herself that the best defense is a good offense.

"Why are you here?" she said.

"Because of Baxter."

Disappointment jolted her. She hoped he didn't see.

"He's doing fine, as you can see."

"He misses his daddy."

B. J. wished he wouldn't keep referring to himself as Baxter's daddy. The picture of him on the floor cavorting and laughing with the Parker children was all too fresh in her mind.

"He has me . . . and my sister Maxie."

"Magic Maxie?"

"You know my sister?" A flash of jealousy ripped through B. J. Good grief, she was turning into a dried-up old witch.

"No, not personally. She's friends with Margaret, my secretary."

Crash picked up Baxter who immediately curled into his lap and went to sleep.

"I want to take Baxter . . ."

"No . . ." B. J. stood up, her knuckles white as she gripped the edge of the desk.

". . . for an occasional outing."

"Oh." B. J. deflated like a pricked balloon.

"I could pick him up occasionally and take him for a spin on the Harley, or a picnic in the park. I might even take him to my house for barbecue. I'm pretty hot with the grill."

Would he want to take her if she looked at him with soulful brown eyes and wagged her tail?

"I see," she said.

"Is that a yes or a no?"

"It's a maybe."

"Good." He stood up, then set the sleeping puppy carefully back onto the chair. Baxter never stirred.

In the doorway he turned back to her.

"When Baxter wakes up, tell him Daddy will be back soon."

She clung to her desk like a honeysuckle vine while he watched her from the doorway. Then he crossed the room in three strides and tipped her face up to his.

Warmth radiated through her, and she felt a tingling deep down in the region of her heart. He was going to kiss her. Not only would she let him, but she would respond.

She waited, breathless, and then he smiled.

"See you later, B. J. Corban."

B. J. made herself stay away from the window until Crash's Harley had roared away down the street. Then she raced across the room for one last glance of him. Everything about him was jaunty and carefree, and she wondered what it would be like to ride off on the back of a Harley.

THIRTEEN

Crash whistled "I'm an Old Cowhand from the Rio Grande," and the wind caught his song and scattered it as he raced through the streets on his Harley. What was it about seeing Philadelphia that always made him want to whistle?

He stopped at a phone booth and called in to his office, then headed home. All the Beauregards except Crash lived in huge homes at ritzy addresses. His house was a pleasant Creole cottage in the country with enough land for horses and goats and cows. He loved animals and never tired of sitting on his back porch looking across the pasture at his small herd of holstein.

As he parked his motorcycle he saw his place through Philadelphia's eyes. She was a city girl; she'd probably hate every minute of being at a place some folks called the back side of nowhere.

Crash didn't know why, but the idea of her not being enchanted with his place made him introspective and somewhat sad. He wasn't accustomed to that either.

"Great Caesar's cupcakes. I've got to put that woman out of my mind."

He called Margaret to check on his calendar, and seeing he would be free for a few days, he packed a knapsack and headed west on his Harley.

Destination unknown.

The doctor's office was crowded with pregnant women. B. J. felt like a cucumber at a watermelon picnic. She riffled through the magazines until she came to one that talked about better homes and gardens instead of better mothers and babies.

A nurse crept to the door in crepe-soled shoes. "B. J. Corban," she announced.

The other women stared at her as she went into the sacred back rooms. B. J. felt guilty, as if she'd won first prize by impersonating somebody.

Somebody pregnant.

Draped in a sheet and a green paper blouse, she watched as the OB/GYN poked and prodded. She shivered. Why were their hands always cold?

Later, sitting in Dr. McKay's office she tried not to fidget.

"You're not pregnant, Miss Corban."

"I know that. . . ." B. J. was not like her sister. She didn't take instantly to strangers, and this man was a stranger to her. She was uncomfortable discussing the most intimate details of her life, even if he was a doctor.

"I just wanted to be sure everything is all right," she added.

"Your lab work is fine. Everything looks good." He polished his glasses. "Are you experiencing any problems that you haven't told me about, Miss Corban?"

"None . . . except every now and then I feel flushed." She didn't tell him that Crash was always around when that happened. "Could it be hot flashes?"

He consulted his records. "It would be most unusual for someone your age to be going through menopause."

"Even prematurely?"

His smile was not unkind. "I'd say you have a few more years."

She felt as if she'd been pardoned from a lifetime prison sentence.

Back at her office she raced to her answering machine. There were two messages, one from a woman answering her ad for a secretary, the other from Mrs. Parker inquiring when they would go to trial.

"Machines do make mistakes," she said, playing the messages again, just to be sure she hadn't missed one.

She hadn't. The plain fact was, Crash hadn't called.

"I'm not going to turn into the kind of woman who hovers over the phone waiting for it to ring," she announced to Baxter as she reached for her mail.

It was scanty by anybody's standards, a flyer from Kroger announcing a special on baked chickens, a check for her work on the first rabbit case, and a letter from her friend and former law partner in Philadelphia.

Gloria's letters were like her, brief and to the point. "I won the Wimsey case, expect big bucks. I got an invitation to a baby shower . . . for Stephen's wife! I chunked it in the garbage can where it belongs. Miss you. Love, Glo."

For no reason at all, B. J. started to cry. Baxter rubbed against her, whining as she tore the letter to bits.

Then she did something she would never have done in Philadelphia: She locked her office and went home in the middle of the day.

Dressed in sweats she curled on the sofa with Baxter on one side and a big bowl of popcorn on the other. *Three Men and a Baby* was playing on the movie channel. B. J. cried through the whole thing.

"I'm going to have a baby," she said.

All trace of tears was scrubbed from B. J.'s face, and she and her sister were in the kitchen fixing supper. Maxie was slicing tomatoes for a salad. She never even paused at B.J.'s announcement. The knife snicked against the cutting board as she continued her dicing.

"When?" Maxie asked.

That question was typical of Maxie. Instead of asking intrusive things such as "Who is the father?", she got down to important things like the date of birth.

"As soon as I can find a suitable father," B. J. said.

"Didn't Grandma ever tell you about the birds and

the bees? I don't think the baby's going to wait around to be born until you can find a suitable father."

B. J. spread mayonnaise on bread, then layered on the cheese and pastrami.

"I'm not pregnant," she said, "at least, not yet."

Maxie put down her carving knife, and wiped her hands on her apron, a frilly pink affair she'd made on the sewing machine she kept in one corner of her bedroom.

"It takes two," she said.

"I know. That's the part that bothers me." B. J. stacked the sandwiches then sliced them in half. "Sperm banks are too impersonal. I want to select my baby's father . . . get to know him personally, at least for a little while."

"It's more fun that way."

"I don't plan to have fun; I just want to get pregnant."

"I thought the two went hand in hand."

"It's not going to be like that. I'm going to select some good breeding stock. . . ." An image of Crash flashed through her mind. His was a great gene pool, and more, so much more. B. J. firmly pushed him from her mind.

"That's where you come in, Maxie."

"Wait a minute. I don't know any good breeding stock. All I know is a few good men."

"I only need one, Maxie." B. J. smiled. "Just one."

———◆———◆———

"This is not the right kind of place, Maxie."

They were at Bogart's, where the music was so loud, B. J. had to scream to be heard. On the small dance floor men in tight jeans danced with women in fringed shirts and cowboy boots. If you could call what they were doing dancing.

"Appearances can be deceiving, B. J. Sometimes there are a few lawyers in this crowd."

"I'll bet. The ones partial to the bottle."

Nonetheless, B. J. scanned the room looking for somebody in a three-piece suit with a briefcase beside the table. A strapping hunk in a muscle shirt winked at her across the room.

That's when she began to have her first doubts about her plan. In theory, it was perfect. She'd find somebody with good genes and a partiality for women with brains. She always skimmed over the next part of her plan, the part known as The Seduction. Years of winning had taught B. J. to focus on results.

And the result of her one-night stand would be a baby who would be exclusively hers, no legal hassles, no commitments, no messy emotional entanglements.

Two of her female friends in Philadelphia had chosen to be single parents. Of course, they'd gone about it differently, but the fact was, single parenthood was a route more and more women in high-powered professions were choosing.

B. J. had always wanted children, and she knew she'd be a good parent. But she wasn't the kind of woman who waited around for nature to take its course.

"I take the bull by the horns," she said.

The band was on a break, and Maxie threw back her head and roared with laughter.

"The bull's coming this way, B. J. And he looks like he might have a twelve-inch horn."

B. J. looked up to see the muscle-bound jock who had winked at her striding in her direction. When he was two tables away she saw the tattoos on his arms, swords and snakes with a fire-breathing dragon thrown in for good measure.

She bolted toward the ladies' room. Maxie found her bent over the toilet heaving.

"Here." Maxie tore off paper towels and handed them to B. J. "In case you need them."

B. J. washed and dried her face. "I knew I shouldn't have worn this red dress," she said. "Red always attracts the wrong kind of man."

"What do you call the right kind of man?"

"Somebody in a starched shirt."

Crash got as far as Arkansas before he realized that riding aimlessly had lost its savor. The sunsets were spectacular, the scenery inviting, the people he met along the way interesting, but something was missing.

Sitting on a picnic bench in a roadside park in Conway, Arkansas watching cardinals picking up crumbs, he understood what was missing. He didn't have anybody to share it with. There was nobody he could turn to and say, "Look at that sky. Did you ever see such color?" or "Does this move toward political correctness make you think of the McCarthy era or the Salem witch hunts?"

He flicked a few crumbs in the direction of the birds. A brilliant male cardinal shooed away a rival male while the duller-feathered female had her turn. He'd heard that cardinals mated for life.

There was a certain beauty in that concept, a certain rightness. If it happened in nature, it couldn't be all bad.

Crash dumped the rest of his lunch into the garbage can, strapped on his helmet, and headed toward home. The closer he got the more excited he became. That had never happened to him before.

On the outskirts of Tupelo he stopped at Ballard Park to do some serious thinking. The Harley scared the ducks on the lake, and they flapped out of the water and hid in the bushes. Crash coaxed them out with bread crumbs, then sat beside the lake wondering what he was going to do next.

The answer wasn't long in coming. He was headed toward Philadelphia. He'd been headed that way all along, maybe ever since he'd met her in the Smokies.

Smiling, he strapped on his helmet and revved his engine. Funny how a woman could get under your skin without your ever knowing it, and then, bingo, all of a sudden the lightbulb comes on and you realize your heart knew it all along.

Baxter recognized the sound of the Harley. He was at the office door barking a full two minutes before

B. J. knew Crash was coming. When she heard him whistling up her walk, she raced to the bathroom and applied lipstick, as flustered as a schoolgirl.

She heard him before she saw him. He came through the door without knocking and his big boom of laughter filled her offices.

"Daddy's home!" he yelled over the sound of joyous barking. "That's my boy. Jump up here and give Daddy a kiss."

Her heart pounded so hard, she pressed her hand over it to calm herself down before she walked into her own reception room. He was tanner than she remembered, blonder, more virile, more handsome. The first thought that ran through her mind was "What a gene pool." The second made her blush.

"Hello, Philadelphia." His eyes raked her boldly over the top of Baxter's head. "You're overdressed for a picnic at the park."

This was typical Crash: show up without calling, snap his fingers, and expect her to jump through a hoop.

"There's a perfectly useful invention called the telephone."

"There are better ways of communicating."

The center of his eyes were so gold, they dazzled her. He set Baxter on his feet, then stalked her. She stood in the doorway waiting. He braced his hands on either side of her, pinning her against the doorframe.

"Shall I show you what they are?" he said, his breath a soft caress against her cheek.

"No." With an effort, she remembered who she

was, who he was. "I don't intend to jeopardize my career over a forbidden tryst with some hotshot judge who thinks he's God's gift to women."

He roared with laughter. "There you go, using those million-dollar words again." He pulled her roughly to him. "I don't have jeopardizing careers in mind, just a simple old-fashioned kiss."

"Let me go," she protested, but not with any conviction. The fact was, she longed for his kiss the way a desert wanderer longed for a cool drink of water.

"I won't even use any tongue, if you say so."

"Neanderthal."

"If the shoe fits . . ."

His smile was slow and easy, his mouth soft and sensual as he lowered it over hers. The kiss touched every part of her body. The heat started in her face, spread down her neck and through her breasts, then ignited her groin and melted her legs. She hung on to him to keep from falling.

He pulled her roughly against his chest as his tongue plundered her mouth. Unable to resist, she traced her hands along the length of his arms and down his back, defining every taut muscle, memorizing every inch of bronzed skin.

His hips pressed provocatively against hers in imitation of a dance her body remembered but her mind refused to acknowledge.

"Did you miss me while I was gone?" he said.

He should be on the stage. Or at the very least in a courtroom trying headline cases. B. J. gathered her wits and untangled herself from his arms.

"Were you gone somewhere, Judge Beaurcgard?"

He laughed. "Philadelphia, someday I'm going to penetrate that armor you hide behind, and when I do, all heaven's going to break loose."

He was so convincing that B. J. was in danger of believing him. And if she believed him, she might start believing in love and promises, in walking down the aisle to pledge vows then going home to raise babies. Judge Nathaniel Bridge "Crash" Beauregard was in danger of dazzling her with hocus-pocus.

She knew all about hocus-pocus. All the best attorneys did. They used it to great effect in the courtroom.

But this was real life. And real life didn't hold out any magic. She was a woman teetering on the brink of menopause who had a solid plan for her future, and she wasn't about to let Crash sidetrack her. No matter how hard he tried.

He tipped her chin up and stared at her in a way that made her want to curl into a ball in his lap and purr.

"You know one of the things I missed most while I was gone?" he said.

"No, but I'm sure you're going to tell me."

"The sting of your waspish tongue."

He made her sound like a spinster shrew.

"I'll try not to deprive you," she said. "I'll leave a sharp message on your answering machine from time to time."

"That won't be necessary. I'm planning on seeing you in person."

"Don't you ever ask?"

"No." He swatted her rump. "Get out of that prissy attitude and those prissy shoes, Philadelphia. We're going for a ride."

The images that came to mind turned her cheeks a bright pink. His chuckle was knowing and wicked.

"Not that kind," he said.

"What kind?" The minute she let her guard down, she knew she'd made a mistake. "Don't answer that."

"Not the kind where we spread a blanket under the stars and get so tangled up with each other we can't tell your body from mine . . . though it does have its merits." He brushed her lips with the tip of his finger. "Do you want me to go into detail, Philadelphia?"

"No . . . I want you to leave. Right now."

"That's what I'm planning to do . . . with you."

"You can take Baxter. I have work to do."

"Nothing that can't wait."

He hung a closed sign on her door, then shut and locked it.

"You can't do that."

"I just did."

She was weakening. It was a glorious day, and she'd had her nose to the grindstone for years. What would one day off hurt?

"What if somebody comes?" she said.

"I've always loved that dirty mind."

Her chair looked small when he sat down in it. He picked up a magazine and started flipping through.

"What are you doing?" she said.

"Don't you worry about a thing, Philadelphia. Your

honor is safe with me." He grinned. "I'm going to guard the door while you change."

"How do you know I have other clothes here?" It was a last-ditch effort to keep from caving in.

"Lawyers like you keep clothes at the office," he said.

It was true. In Philadelphia she'd worked such long hours that she would never have been able to go anywhere at night if she'd had to fight her way through the traffic in order to go home and change. Though her client list in Tupelo was still small, she kept up her old habits. Sort of. She wasn't working the long hours yet, but she still had clothes at the office.

"I'll go for just a little while," she said, "but only in order to keep my eye on Baxter."

He could hear the sounds she made as she changed clothes, the soft snick of a zipper, the sensual swishing of silk against silk. Sitting in the chair was almost more temptation than he could bear.

Crash shifted to make his jeans more comfortable, and held his ground. He'd never courted a woman before. As silly as that sounded, it was true. All his relationships had been casual. He'd fallen into them without effort, and out again with equal ease.

He had no idea how to proceed with Philadelphia. The only thing he knew for sure was that he had to. Joe would be no help at all. Though his brother was engaged, Crash had no intention of trying to imitate something that seemed more like contract negotiations than romance.

"I'm ready," she said.

Philadelphia stood in the doorway looking softer and more feminine than he'd ever seen her. It was something about the eyes. Desire smacked him so hard, he actually had to sit awhile in order to collect himself.

"We're riding on the Harley," he said.

"I've had one ride with you."

Color bloomed across her cheeks. Memories of the ride washed over him, her arms around his chest, her breasts pressed into his back. If he had it to do all over again, he'd have let nature take its course in the mountains.

But now it was too late. Circumstances forced him into this awkward position of having to think before he acted, having to weigh each word to know if it was the right thing.

"Don't be afraid, Philadelphia."

"I'm not afraid," she added, licking her lips.

He was. He was scared witless. For a moment he was tempted to bolt, to jump on his motorcycle and head home where he could hole up in his cottage and do some serious thinking.

Instinct told him all the thinking in the world wouldn't change the facts: He wanted the woman in the doorway, and he wanted her on a level he'd never known, wanted her in a way he could hardly understand, let alone articulate.

"Your steed awaits," he said.

They walked out arm in arm, Fred Astaire and Ginger Rogers before they began a slow, sweet tango.

FOURTEEN

There were ducks at the park, and children racing after red and yellow balls. Baxter was in his element, and so was Crash.

Every time B. J. looked in his direction, he had another child on his shoulders or clinging to his hands or tugging at his pants leg. At the moment he was pawing in the grass pretending to be a bull while two little boys swung make-believe swords and pretended to be bullfighters.

He caught her watching and gave her a wicked grin.

"Don't you want to come down here and be an animal?"

He made her want to be an animal, all right, but not with an audience.

"I'll leave that to you. You do it so well."

"It comes from lots of experience."

He dusted the grass off his pants and stretched out beside her on the park bench, deliciously male and outrageously appealing. She braced herself for another battle of wits, but he did something so unexpected, it took her breath away.

"Even an animal can change his stripes," he said, and then he lifted her left hand to his lips and planted a kiss in her palm, a kiss so soft, so tender that she almost cried.

Instead she jumped up and hugged her dog to her chest.

"We'd better take Baxter home. He's had enough excitement for one day."

Crash tipped her chin up with two fingers. "How about you, Philadelphia? Have you had enough for one day?"

That's all it took from him, one single touch and she melted.

"More than enough." She licked her lips, and he studied her face as if he were committing it to memory. And then he did another totally unexpected thing: He let her go without further comment, then took her home and left her with a friendly peck on the cheek.

"I wonder what he meant about an animal changing its stripes," she said.

Baxter was too tuckered out to answer.

"Are you almost dressed, B. J.?" Maxie called, then swept through the bedroom door. Draped in a white feather boa and wearing a white silk dress cut on the bias, she looked like a movie star straight from the forties. All she needed was a rhinestone tiara and a cigarette holder to complete the image.

Standing in her black silk teddy and black silk stockings, B. J. looked at the red dress lying on the bed. The seduction dress, Maxie called it.

"Good grief, B. J. Hurry up. We're going to be late."

"I'm not so sure about this, Maxie. After all, I'm trying to establish myself as a respectable lawyer in this town."

"Is there any such thing?"

B. J. threw a stocking at Maxie, then pursed her lips and went to her closet. She rummaged through until she found her old standby, a black cocktail dress, high-necked and sedate, completely without ornamentation.

"You're not wearing that!"

"Why not?" B. J. laid the dress on the bed, then began to rummage for a pair of sensible shoes. "It's a perfectly respectable dress, exactly right for the professional image I want to create."

"What's that? Sourpuss in mourning?"

"Face it, Maxie. There are all kinds of people in this world, and some of us happen to look, act, and dress conservatively."

Maxie picked up the dress, made a face, then dropped it back onto the bed.

"But what about your plan? What about the baby?"

B. J. felt as if she'd been gut punched. Out of the corner of her eye she caught a glimpse of herself in Maxie's pier mirror. Was that a new line showing around her mouth?

"Time marches on," Maxie said, goading her.

Each day brought a new line, a new sign of aging. Before B. J. knew it, time would have marched right past her, leaving her old and dried up, past the age of childbearing.

"Remember what Grandma used to say?"

"Maxie . . ."

" 'Remember, girls, you're Corbans. A Corban always fights for what she wants.' " Maxie paused.

" 'If something's not worth fighting for, it's not worth having,' " B. J. added.

Going to the bed, she picked up the red dress, then held it to her chest.

"Atta girl," Maxie said.

"Still, I don't think this red dress is right for tonight."

"If you're going to lure a stud into your bed, you've got to show a little of the merchandise."

"For Pete's sake, Maxie. This is a banquet for Tupelo's business leaders. I doubt if a single one of them will qualify for the role of *stud*."

With one notable exception.

"Then why are we going there? I know a little lounge where some really great people hang out, theater people, artsy types. . . . I'd sort of like my niece to be born with talent."

Trust Maxie to decide the baby's sex in advance.

"We're going because it's a civic duty," B. J. said.

And because at the park Crash had casually mentioned that he would be there. "One night of torture per year is the extent of my civic duty," he'd said.

B. J. zipped herself into the red dress then pulled at the top, trying to cover more of her breasts.

"Besides, if I'm going to be successful in this town, I have to become a presence."

"After tonight, you'll be a presence they'll never forget."

B. J. looked down at her left thigh showing boldly through the slit skirt. "That's what I'm afraid of."

Maxie plucked a pair of rhinestone earrings from her jewelry box on the dressing table. "Here. Wear these. Gild the lily."

"If I gild this lily any more, I'm afraid it will tarnish." She handed the earrings back to Maxie.

"Think of your cause, B. J. Think of the baby." Maxie attached the earrings to her sister's ears. "Men go for tarnished women."

Heads turned when the Corban sisters walked into the banquet hall.

"Everybody's staring," B. J. said.

"It's good for business." Maxie smiled and waved at everybody, whether she knew them or not.

"Yours maybe, but not mine. I'm supposed to be a *lawyer*, for Pete's sake."

"I wasn't talking about your law practice. I'm talking about Operation Motherhood."

Maxie plucked two glasses of wine off a table as they passed, and handed one to B. J.

"If you're going to . . ." Maxie stopped in midsentence. "Good grief. I've found him."

"Who?"

B. J. turned to look in the direction Maxie was staring. There he was, as bold as brass and twice as showy, Judge Nathaniel Bridge Beauregard, making a white shirt and tie look as rakish as pirate's garb.

"The man of your dreams," Maxie said, still staring. "Good grief, wouldn't you like to melt his starch?"

A flash of pure jealousy went through B. J. Crash would look up and see Maxie, and bells would ring all over the building. She was exactly his type, untamed and untamable, as wild as they came. Maxie gave new meaning to the word *unconventional*.

"He's not my type," B. J. said.

And then she drained half her glass. Never mind that she had a low tolerance for alcohol. Never mind that she could get knee-walking drunk on only one glass. What the heck? Her biological clock was ticking so loudly, it sounded like a time bomb. If she didn't soon find a candidate for father-of-the-baby, she might as well hang up her red dress and go calmly into spinsterhood.

She took another long swig of wine. "Besides," she said. "I don't like blonds."

"Blonds? I'm not talking about the blond. It's that dark-headed hunk beside him that I'm talking about."

B. J. hadn't seen anybody except Crash. But that's the way it always was. He dominated a room, making everything and everybody else seem insignificant.

She glanced in his direction again. A tall, distinguished looking man stood beside Crash. Dark hair, dark eyes, well built, nice looking, sexy in a subtle kind of way. He wasn't Crash, but he wasn't half bad.

"Come on," Maxie said.

"Where are you going?"

"To meet Mr. Perfect."

B. J. had a sudden vision of herself in her red dress, trying to seduce a father for her child right under the amused gaze of Judge Nathaniel Beauregard.

"I don't think he's the right one," B. J. protested, but Maxie was barreling straight ahead in her usual manner. There was no telling what kind of trouble she'd get them both into if B. J. didn't trail along. Besides, the man Maxie called Mr. Perfect was the only one with potential B. J. had seen.

Feeling wobbly from the wine and tawdry from the dress, she marched toward Crash to the rhythm of her steadily ticking biological clock. He took in everything she had with one sweeping glance.

"Philadelphia . . ." He assessed her once more, and she flushed under that bold, hot gaze. "I haven't seen this much of you since the Smokies."

"You must be Crash." Maxie said, her attention not on him but on the man at his side.

"Judge Nathaniel Bridge Beauregard," B. J. said. "In the living flesh."

"I was going to say the same thing about you," Crash said, his eyes fixed to the neckline of her dress.

Maybe the wine made her reckless, or maybe it was desperation. Whatever it was, B. J. didn't think twice, she merely reacted. Turning toward the man beside Crash she took a deep breath so that her breasts were presented like ripe plums on a platter, their nipples hard as diamonds underneath the thin silky fabric.

The man beside Crash raised an eyebrow. Good. She'd caught his attention. Maybe Maxie was right. Maybe he *was* the perfect man. Up close B. J. could see no flaws.

"Come here, Philadelphia. . . ." Crash's arm snaked out, and he pulled her roughly to his side. She didn't dare look at him. Sweat popped out on her upper lip. She'd never been one of those women who didn't sweat. The next thing she knew it would be running down her cheeks and through her cleavage.

Under the innocent guise of holding her, Crash slid his fingers under her arm and massaged the side of her breast. He'd made it perfectly clear that he didn't want her, so what was he trying to prove now?

Angry at him, at herself, at the whole situation, B. J. wet her lips with the tip of her tongue and gave the man beside Crash her most dazzling smile. She wasn't sure he noticed, he was so busy watching Maxie.

Crash's fingers never stopped their secret, erotic massage.

"I think you should get to know this man you're trying so hard to vamp," he said. Darn him. Why didn't he just go away?

"Philadelphia, meet Attorney at Law Joseph Patrick Beauregard."

She stiffened as if she'd been prodded with a hot poker. "Beauregard?"

"My brother." Crash's grin was wicked. She wanted to kill him.

Wasn't that just her luck? The only man in the room with father potential turned out to be Crash's brother. Even if she could seduce him, Crash would be her baby's uncle. Not that she stood a ghost of a chance with Maxie on the premises. Joseph Beauregard was looking at her as if she might be something he planned to put on a silk pillow and ply with cream from a saucer.

Before B. J. could decide what to do, a woman with hair like polished copper and the reflexes of a coiled snake cut Maxie and B. J. off from Joseph P. Beauregard.

"Darling . . . ," she said, draping herself over his arm.

"My fiancée," he said.

Neither of them could remember her name. Later, sitting two tables away, still flushed with wine and the nearness of Crash, B. J. tried to cut into her rubbery chicken.

"Who did he say she was?" Maxie asked.

"I don't remember."

"She looks like a cold fish to me."

"I didn't notice."

"Not the type for him at all."

"How could you tell? You don't even know him."

"That can easily be remedied. . . . We'll mingle after the speaker or . . . I've got it . . . We'll invite them back to the house for cocktails after dinner."

"Forget it, Maxie. Mr. Perfect is not for me."

"Oh, I couldn't agree with you more. He's too . . . perfect." Maxie sighed.

B. J. studied her sister. Maxie was not the kind who sighed over men: Men always sighed over her. B. J.'s big-sister instincts took over.

"Maxie, don't you dare start getting ideas over a man who is already taken. Especially not tonight. All I want to do is get out of here and get out of this dress."

"Relax. You look smashing. Crash thought so too."

"How could you tell?" B. J. was pleased in spite of herself.

"Look at the eyes. What a man thinks of you is always in his eyes."

B. J. glanced at his table, but Crash was deep in conversation with his brother. If he even knew where she was sitting, she couldn't tell.

"Not that it matters. All I want to do is go home."

Maxie set her glass down with such force, the silver rattled.

"You can't quit now, B. J. Just look around you." Maxie gestured toward the tables that held Tupelo's elite. "It's a regular sperm bank out there."

"What am I supposed to do? Walk up to somebody and say, 'I like your genes. Hand over your sperm.'" She attacked her chicken as if it might fight back. "Maybe it's a sperm bank out there, but I'm not cut out to be a bank robber."

"You're not giving up? B. J., you can't quit. You're not a quitter."

"Yes, I am." B. J. took a long slug of wine. Her

second glass. "I quit the altar and I'm quitting the father search."

Maxie pulled out a tissue and silently handed it across the table. Equally silent, B. J. took it. She sniffled discreetly, then felt a flood coming on.

"Excuse me," she said, then bolted toward the ladies' room.

Halfway there she decided that banquet halls were designed by the same people who created mazes. She felt like a rat, doomed to wander endlessly.

Suddenly there was a hand on her elbow, and she looked up to see Crash.

"Don't say anything," he said. "Just keep walking."

For once she didn't argue.

He guided her through the tables, around the corner, and out the back door. She leaned against the wall, the tissue wadded in her hand.

"Where's the ladies' room?" she said.

"You don't have to hide in a ladies' room to cry. You can cry on my shoulder."

"I'm not crying."

"So I see." He pulled a handkerchief out of his pocket and dabbed at her cheeks.

"Thanks," she said. "Sometimes you're not half bad."

The cool night breeze dried the rest of her tears, and just when she thought she had herself under control, she looked at Crash in the moonlight. He was everything she wanted the father of her child to be, strong and handsome, cheerful and witty, intelligent and personable.

He pulled a pipe from his pocket and lit it, never taking his eyes off hers. His riveting stare caught her high up under the breastbone, and she could hardly breathe. He blew a perfect smoke ring, then a second and a third, his eyes gleaming with an unholy light.

Her skin caught fire. "What?" she finally said.

He took the pipe from his mouth. "You tried to seduce my brother."

She didn't bother to deny it.

He reached out and drew his finger along the top of her plunging neckline, leaving a trail of goose bumps on her skin. Slowly, he retraced his path, pausing long enough to delve briefly into her cleavage.

She stood perfectly still. She'd been through this before with him. Crash loved to take her to the brink, then back off.

"What I want to know is why?" The soft silkiness of his voice disguised the steel underneath.

Reeling with wine and conflicting emotions, B. J. closed her eyes to shut out the sight of him. What was the use of torturing herself? He didn't want her except as something to toy with.

"B. J. . . ." He caught her face between his hands and tipped her face upward. "Look at me." She opened her eyes slowly, like somebody waking from a dream. "Why did you try to seduce my brother?"

Even now, knowing Crash didn't want her, she was so hot and ready for him, she could hardly stand. She clenched her shaking hands into fists and jerked out of reach.

"What do you care?"

She stalked toward the banquet hall. Inside was a sea of white linen tablecloths and white starched shirts gleaming in the candlelight. Somewhere across that vast sea was Maxie. B. J. felt as if she were drowning with not a single lifeboat in sight.

She had gained the vestibule when Crash scooped her up and strode off into the darkness.

"Put me down."

"Not a chance."

She drew back her fist, and he laughed.

"Fight, Philadelphia. Let's see your left hook."

She folded her hands across her chest and glared at him.

"I wouldn't give you the pleasure."

Chuckling, he carried her across the parking lot. In the glow of streetlights his Harley looked as menacing as the warrior himself.

Holding her against his chest, he straddled the seat and revved the engine.

"Where are you taking me?"

"Home."

"I don't have a home."

"I do."

She had a mental image: a cozy fire and moonlight streaming through the window, a patchwork quilt and legs entwined, soft music and whispered words in the darkness.

What she meant to say was, "Not on your life." What she said instead was, "Hmmm."

And what she did was snuggle closer to his chest.

His jaw clenched, and he squeezed her so hard, she almost lost her breath.

Was it possible she could seduce him? Would it be possible to use him for one night and then never see him again?

If she'd had all her faculties about her, she'd have taken out a notebook and listed the pros and cons. The cons would surely have outweighed the pros, and she'd have cast off her notion as not only foolish but also dangerous.

But she was full of wine and recklessness. Circling her arms around his neck she drew him close. His breath made her skin hot, and even if she'd wanted to turn back it was already too late, far too late.

"Crash . . ."

"Hmm?"

"There's something I want you to do."

The moonlight caught in his hair and his eyes, and he looked like a god descended from Mount Olympus for the express purpose of cavorting with mortals. She'd never felt more mortal . . . or more vulnerable.

He quirked an eyebrow upward.

"Not yet," she said.

As he roared out of the parking lot, her internal clock struck the hour. A quarter till midnight. She had to hurry before it was too late.

FIFTEEN

The madness that drove him was jealousy, pure unadulterated jealousy. And of his own brother. As he zipped along in the night, he mentally kicked himself.

He was turning into somebody he didn't know, somebody he didn't even like. Jealousy, kidnapping. What would he resort to next?

There was no question about it. What he was doing was tantamount to kidnapping, and kidnapping was no way to conduct a courtship. And it was certainly no way to tell the woman in his arms that she was important to him. More than important. Necessary in ways he'd never dreamed possible.

He veered left off the highway onto a gravel driveway that meandered through a hundred-year-old pecan grove. At the end of the driveway was his cottage, nestled among the magnolias and camellias and gardenias as if it had sprung up from the rich soil in the flower garden.

Crash never failed to get a rush of pleasure from the sight of his house. He searched Philadelphia's face, anxious for her reaction.

"You live here?" she said.

It wasn't what he expected, but he could live with the disappointment. After all, she was a big-city girl. A man couldn't have everything.

"Yes. I live here."

She stood on the front porch, closed her eyes, and drew a deep breath.

"It smells like a place you would live . . . an extravagance of wildness and freedom." She smiled. "I like it."

"You always surprise me, Philadelphia."

"I'm a big-city girl by choice, but I grew up in the country. On a farm, as a matter of fact . . . a place very much like this. Do you have animals?"

"Yes. Listen."

In the distance they heard the plaintive whinny of a horse, then an answering snort and the thundering of hooves across the pasture.

"It's mating season," he said.

She stiffened, and then she transformed before his eyes. Everything about her became liquid, her eyes, her smile, even her bones. She slithered across the porch and wrapped herself around him, then clung there like a morning-glory vine.

"So it is," she said.

She spoke in a voice he'd never heard her use, a soft seductive whisper that sent shivers over him. Then she nuzzled his neck and actually purred. The behavior was so uncharacteristic of her that he was thrown completely off guard.

Not that he didn't like it. On the contrary, he found this unexpectedly sensual side of Philadelphia to be extraordinarily appealing. What man could resist?

He scooped her up and carried her across his threshold, just like a hero in the late-night movie classics he loved to watch. It was an image of himself that he enjoyed.

His courtship was advancing far faster than he'd imagined.

"How about some music," he said.

"Music?"

Moonlight laid a path from the window to the doorway, and Philadelphia's eyes were as luminous as a cat's. She made that little noise again, half purr, half growl, and then she began to nibble his neck.

He was so excited, he couldn't even find the light switch. Great Caesar's aphrodisiac. Goose bumps the size of golf balls popped up on his skin. He'd never known it was possible to have such a reaction to the touch of a woman.

He found the sofa in the dark. It was a man's couch, big and roomy with lots of puffy pillows. He placed her among the pillows, carefully lest he break the spell that bound them. She was lush and inviting, her lips a slash of scarlet, pouty and ripe, her breasts soft creamy globes rising above her low-slung neckline, one silken thigh completely exposed, the other a rich curve underneath the silky red dress.

"Come here," she whispered, lifting her arms, and

he fell into them, a man possessed, so hungry for what she offered that he forgot how he'd meant to court her, forgot about the candlelight and soft music, forgot the fire he'd meant to build in the grate, just enough to take the spring chill out of the air and send a pleasant cozy glow over the room.

He forgot everything except the rich pleasure of her lips and the ripe promise of her body. She murmured and writhed as he kissed her, spurring him on until he could barely keep from ripping aside her dress and plunging into her like the stallion that rutted and pawed in his pasture.

"You are delicious," he whispered.

"Don't talk. . . ." She pulled him down hard against her. "Just don't talk."

He was so ready for her he thought he would explode. But even as his passion mounted, something deep inside him whispered caution; something he'd only lately discovered to be his heart yearned for the tender words, the sweet, slow buildup, the commitment.

He thrust his tongue into her mouth and engaged hers in a provocative duel. Even though desire wound him as tightly as a bowstring, he could still think about such heady stuff as commitment. Funny how'd he'd always thought the only thing he wanted was freedom. Even after he met Philadelphia he didn't know how hard he'd fallen; he didn't understand that freedom meant enjoying all the things life had to offer, including love.

Joe would laugh his head off if he knew Crash's

dilemma: The man who had always enjoyed the pleasures of a woman's body without any thought beyond the moment now found himself being used in the same way, being used and wishing for the powerful, magical bonds of love and commitment.

Cupping her face, he came up for air. In the moonlight she was beautifully disheveled and incredibly desirable.

"Philadelphia . . ."

"Hmmm?"

She licked one finger and traced his lips while thrusting her hips boldly against his. He nearly exploded.

"I thought a small fire would be nice, and maybe some slow sexy blues."

"What's the matter, Crash?" She reached for his shirt buttons. "Getting cold feet again?"

"Again?"

"Just like in the Smokies. All bluster and no performance."

"Is that what this is to you? A performance?"

She parted his shirt and raked her fingernails down his chest, never stopping the urgent, undulating rhythm of her hips.

"Spoken just like a lawyer," she said. "Always analyzing."

In a neat role reversal she was skewering him with his own sword. All that aside, she was seducing him as he'd never been seduced. Only a man of iron would be immune to her sexual overtures, and he'd never laid claim to such a dubious fame.

He pushed aside the top of her dress to expose her nipples. Taking his time he bathed each one thoroughly with his tongue, then took the left one deep in his mouth and sucked until she was groaning.

"Is this what you want, Philadelphia?"

"Yes . . . oh, yes." She pulled his head down. "More."

"That's an invitation too good to resist."

He paid rapt attention to each breast, toying and teasing with fingertips, licking and sucking until she was incoherent with hunger.

She had nothing on him. He was almost incoherent himself.

"You're wearing too many clothes, Philadelphia."

"Why don't you take them off?"

Tangled together on the sofa he struggled to reach her zipper. Impatient, she shoved him aside, then stood in the path of moonlight and shed her dress with the finesse of a high-class call girl. Just looking at her made him so hard, he hurt. A black lace teddy hugged her curves, and black silk stockings attached to a garter belt encased her long slim legs. She still wore her heels, sling-back pumps with a saucy satin bow, naughty shoes that begged a man to do all manner of erotic things.

"You're incredible," he said.

She pushed her straps down over her shoulders to completely expose her breasts. Then lifting them in her palms like sacrificial offerings, she whispered, "Do you want them?"

"Yes."

"They're yours."

He left a trail of clothes as he walked toward her. Then, bending over her, took them into his mouth once more.

He reached for her straps, but she stopped him.

"No . . . not like that."

She reached for his shaft, slid her hands along its rigid length, then stepped out of his reach. It was exquisite torture.

"Like this," she said, unsnapping her teddy.

He sank to his knees to take what she offered. She tangled her hands in his hair and held on while he feasted on the sweet, hot juices.

"You taste so good," he said. "So good."

Drunk with her taste, he lowered her to the rug and pressed the tip of his shaft against her slick, swollen sex.

"Is this what you want?" He slid the tip of his shaft along her hot folds, barely edging in, then pulling out. It took every ounce of control not to bury himself to the hilt in her and spew his seed in one long, explosive burst.

"Yes, I want it . . . now, Crash . . . now." She thrust upward, taking him fully inside.

It was too quick, too fast. He wanted a long, sweet meandering journey. He wanted to discover her secret erotic spots slowly, one by one, taking the time to comment, to savor, to memorize.

But she was thrusting against him so insistently, he got caught up in her hard, fast rhythm.

"You're a stallion," she whispered, "a magnificent stud."

The fit was perfect; the feel was magic. Love welled up inside him and spilled over. Each thrust was straight from his heart, each touch directly from his soul.

"Philadelphia, I . . ."

Never ceasing her fierce rhythm, she covered his mouth with her hands.

"Now, Crash. *Now.*"

How easy it would be. Just let go and spurt his juice with the abandon of a wild animal.

But he wanted more . . . ever so much more.

"Not yet." He eased back, partially withdrawing.

"No . . ." She wrapped her legs around him and pulled him back down. "Please . . . please."

"I'm not leaving." He caressed her cheek, her eyebrows, the side of her nose. "I'm just slowing things down a little, prolonging the pleasure."

"I don't . . . want . . . pleasure . . . I want . . ."

Alarm bells went off. Philadelphia had been as elusive as the deer of the Smoky Mountains. If he had been thinking with his head instead of his heart, he might have questioned her astonishing reversal.

"What do you want, Philadelphia?"

She wet her lips with the tip of her tongue, drawing a slow, sensual circle. He almost died.

"You," she whispered. "I want you."

He studied her, the flushed face, the bruised, pouty looking lips, the shining eyes. She was by far the most complex woman he'd ever known. Every time he thought he had her figured out, she made him see how

wrong he was. It would take the rest of his life to un-
ravel the mystery of her, every day, every hour, every
minute to decipher the exciting puzzle of her.

Hunger gnawed at his loins, passion rode his back
like a tiger, but there was something missing, something vital. He thrust his shaft deeply into her, impaling her. She clung to him, gasping.

"Why?" he whispered. He held her arms above her
head and began a slow, teasing rhythm, tantalizing her,
tantalizing himself. "Why do you want me?"

"Oh, God . . . please . . ."

He held very still, and she arched hard against him,
twisting and turning.

"Please . . . Crash . . . please . . . now . . . *Now*."

He was so close to letting go, so close.

"Not yet," he whispered, pumping hard against
her. "Not . . . yet."

Sweat slicked his back and poured down the side of
his face. With a control he'd never have dreamed possible he pounded into her as if he could drive the truth
from her with the fury of his lovemaking.

"Yes," she murmured. "Yes, yes, yes." Almost
mindless, she met him thrust for thrust, writhing
and moaning. "Yes . . . like that . . . Crash . . .
deep . . . plant it deep."

Surrounded by her hot flesh, buried so deep, he felt
as if he had thrust all the way to her heart, pulsing so
hard, he felt as if he were going to erupt with volcanic
force, he held himself still and studied her.

He knew that look. It wasn't the soft look of a
woman fulfilled, but the squared-jaw look of a deter-

mined woman with a quest. What was she after? Surely not revenge. Surely not paying him back for what she considered a spurning in the mountains.

Philadelphia was many things, but she was not petty.

"Plant what deep?" he said.

"Please."

"Please what?"

She clutched him hard against her chest, her jaw set. "Do I have to beg?"

"Beg for what?"

"You know."

"No. Tell me. You're a lawyer, you know how to get what you want." He rammed into her so hard, she sucked in her breath. "What do you want, Philadelphia?"

"You."

"You've got that." He pulled slowly back, then rammed again. She arched, then held herself high, suspended on his shaft. "What else do you want?"

Their eyes locked; their wills clashed. The moon illuminated them . . . the rivers of sweat on his face and his back, her naked breasts with nipples as hard as apricot seeds, the black teddy twisted down around her slender waist, her silk-stockinged legs spread and willing, her high heels planted firmly on the floor.

She was the first to move.

She began an urgent rhythm, milking him, trying his control.

He almost lost it.

"Wait . . . Philadelphia . . . wait . . . let me get some protection."

"Don't worry about it."

She thrust recklessly, wantonly. He felt himself tumbling over the cliff, dying the slow, sweet death.

"Are you protected?" he asked, easing back to gain control.

She glared at him, panting. "Damn you . . . Crash . . . plant . . . your . . . *seed.*"

Rocked to the very core of his being, he withdrew. On hands and knees he stared down at her.

"What are you trying to do?" he said.

She bit her lip, and tears sprang to her eyes.

"You wanted to get pregnant. . . . Is that it?"

It was an age-old ploy: bait the trap, set it, and when the baby's in the oven, slam the door shut. Many women before her had tried it. And yet . . .

He studied her . . . the strong jaw, the clear, steady gaze, the determined face. She was a brilliant woman, not at all the kind who would stoop to such a dirty trick.

"Please get off me," she said.

"Not yet." He held her arms pinned above her head. "Not till I learn the truth."

She didn't fight against him, but merely lay on the rug as expressionless and stiff as a department store mannequin.

"There's nothing more to say," she said.

It couldn't be rejection she was feeling, not after the way he'd given in to unbridled passion. There was something else, something he was missing.

He thought back over all their encounters, tried to remember anything that would give him a clue to her behavior. Though she kept surprising him, she'd been consistent up until tonight: She was basically a hard-working conservative lawyer who tried to hide her soft spot behind a rapier wit.

But tonight she'd let her hair down and dressed for seduction. Why?

Tonight she'd flaunted herself before a group of Tupelo's most conservative, most socially prominent people. Why?

Tonight she'd brazenly flirted with his brother. No, more than flirted. She'd tried to seduce him.

The truth hit Crash with the force of a falling meteor.

"You *do* want a baby," he said.

Her face was a dead giveaway. For a fleeting moment she looked so wistful and dewy-eyed, he almost pulled her into his lap and cradled her like a child. Then he remembered her perfidy.

"You were using me," he added.

"That's right. I was using you."

He'd hoped she would deny it, even if it were true. Hearing her admit the truth hurt more than he cared to think about.

She struggled then, struggled to free herself from his grasp and get off the rug, but he held her fast.

In spite of everything he still wanted her. In spite of his bruised and battered ego, he still loved her.

She glared at him, her eyes shooting sparks. He felt

his passion stir anew, and naked, there was no way to disguise it.

She gave no sign of emotion except the slight tremor in her voice. "I wouldn't have your baby if you were the last man on earth."

"You wouldn't have my baby, period. Not under these conditions."

"Let me up."

"I'm not done with you yet."

"If you touch me, I'll scream."

"It's a little late for that, isn't it?"

She struggled briefly, then made herself go limp. "Cretin."

He laughed, but it was without mirth. "Looks like we're back where we started, Philadelphia."

Before she could catch herself, her face softened. A man looking with his heart can see many things, and what he saw was a combination of regret, nostalgia, and longing. And as much as he wanted a little taste of revenge for what she had done, he couldn't bring himself to punish her further.

He brushed her dark, damp hair off her forehead tenderly, in the way of a man who loves a woman.

"When I have a baby, Philadelphia, it will be with a woman I love . . . a woman I treasure more than my freedom and my Harley . . . a woman who can skewer me with a word and melt me with a single teardrop, a woman who thinks she hates nature but who embraces a lost shaggy dog as if it were her child. . . . *If* I love a woman . . ."

B. J. sucked in a sharp breath, and her eyes searched

his. He stood up and silently offered her his hand. She caught hold, then stood beside him, her teddy still off her shoulders, the snaps undone, her face devoid of makeup, and her hair tumbling over her naked shoulders.

He'd never wanted her more. Nor loved her more.

"Crash . . ."

"Get dressed, Philadelphia. I'm taking you home."

SIXTEEN

She didn't even know Crash owned a car. It was a sturdy Lincoln, not at all the kind of car she'd have pictured him having. It was the kind of car a man with a wife and four children would use, the kind of car that would go to church and PTA meetings and library lectures. Not that any of that mattered. She was glad she didn't have to ride home on the back of the Harley. She was grateful for the spacious front seat that allowed her to hug the door on her side without having so much as the hem of her skirt touch him.

It was a silent drive home, and all the way she prayed Maxie wouldn't be waiting up for her. She prayed that she'd be able to hold back her tears until she could gain the safety of the narrow bed in the guest bedroom.

Then she planned to cry till next Tuesday. Or maybe longer. Maybe she'd never stop.

The only time Crash spoke to her was to ask directions.

"Maxwell Street," she said. "The yellow house."

He parked out front, then came around to open her door. He didn't offer his hand, and she didn't touch him. They didn't even say good-bye.

It was just as well. If she'd had to tell him good-bye, she'd have cried right there on the street, right in front of Crash and the neighbors and God and everybody.

A lamp burned in the den, and Maxie sat curled in her pink chair, sewing glasses on the end of her nose and a piece of needlepoint in her lap. She glanced up from her sewing when B. J. came through the door.

"What in the world . . . You look like you've been run over by a Mack truck or worse."

"Worse." B. J. took off her shoes and walked toward her bedroom in stocking feet. " 'Night, Maxie."

"Wait a minute . . . You can't just go to bed and leave me hanging. Where did you go? I saw Crash follow you out. Were you with him?"

"I don't want to talk about it."

Maxie had a sixth sense that told her when not to argue. She picked up her needlework and started stitching with a fury.

B. J. looked at her sister curled in the plush chair like a doll somebody had forgotten to put to bed. When they were little, B. J. was the one who had tucked her in. Maxie wouldn't go to sleep without telling everything that had happened to her that day. She had a knack for making each event seem like the most fascinating adventure or the most horrible crisis in the world.

After she'd finished a recital of her day, she would cock her head to one side, look at B. J. with her big blue eyes and say, "Now, tell your day."

They had held nothing back from each other. But they were no longer children. Life was no longer simple.

Her stockings made a swishing sound on the carpet, the bedroom seemed a million miles away, and suddenly B. J. needed the comfort and security of a familiar routine.

"Maxie . . ."

Maxie took one look at her, then raced out of the chair to embrace B. J.

"Come over here . . ." Maxie led her to the sofa, then sat down beside her and caressed her hair as if she were a child. "It's going to be all right."

B. J. leaned into her sister. "I want to tell my day," she whispered.

The sisters looked at each other, then Maxie grinned.

"Is this going to be a long story?"

"A very long story."

"I'll make tea."

Tears pushed their way to the surface, and B. J. didn't even try to stop them. Maxie came back with two cups of tea and a box of tissues. B. J. sobbed through the entire first cup.

Maxie refilled their cups, then sat in her pink chair and took up her needlepoint.

"Talk whenever you're ready," she said.

"What are you making?" B. J. asked.

Maxie held up the needlework. *Take the risk and the angels come* was stitched in bright pink, and around the slogan danced fairies and elves in leaf hats, cats and dogs in tutus, elephants and zebras in garlands and crowns, all in vivid, glow-in-the-dark colors. It had all the hallmarks of a Maxie original.

"For you," she said. "For the nursery."

B. J. pressed the tissue over her mouth to stifle a sob, then blew her nose and took a long sip of tea.

"There's not going to be a nursery—not now, not ever."

"Things can't be that bad."

"I've made a complete mess of my life. I've lost everything that was important to me."

"You're probably overreacting. I know you're older and wiser and smarter than I am, but you do tend to overreact, B. J."

"If you're going to sit there and pass judgment, I'm going to bed where I can wallow in my misery in peace."

B. J. slammed the cup into the saucer with the intent of stalking off, then broke out in a fresh gale of weeping.

"Good grief . . ." Maxie went to the kitchen and came back with another box of tissues and a plate of brownies.

"Here, chocolate always makes me feel better." Maxie passed the plate, and B. J. took two. "I'm going to horsewhip that man. What did he do to you, B. J.?"

"That's just the problem . . . he didn't do anything."

"Nothing?"

"Not what I wanted, at least."

Maxie completely lost interest in her brownie. "No, you didn't. Don't tell me you decided to use *Crash* as the father of your baby."

"It was horrible, absolutely horrible."

"Was he *that* bad?"

"No! He was magnificent."

"Magnificent?"

"Oh . . . Maxie." Her sister's name came out as a wail.

"What in the world happened?"

B. J. blew her nose. It was time to face the truth.

"I tried to use the man I love," she whispered.

"I can't believe I'm hearing this. Are we talking about the same man? The one you met in the mountains? The one you scathingly refer to as Tarzan on a Harley?"

She remembered how he'd first looked on his Harley, like a magnificent beast in need of taming. Was that the moment she fell in love with him? Or was it the night she'd wallowed on him naked then stood in the rain with him cuddling a frazzled little puppy? Or was it when he'd kissed her in his judicial robe? Surely it was before tonight, for the moment he'd entered her she knew, knew without a shadow of a doubt that only one man could possibly feel so perfect—the man she loved. He hadn't merely penetrated her body; he'd penetrated her heart and soul. And she'd wanted him as she'd never wanted another man. True, she'd begged for his seed, but not merely because she'd wanted a baby. Too late she'd realized she wanted to be a part of him, wanted him to be a part of her.

Because of love. Only because of love.

"He's magical, Maxie," she whispered. "And I never knew I loved him until it was too late."

"It's never too late, B. J."

"Yes, it is."

Maxie passed the plate once more.

"Have another brownie. If you really love him, we'll think of a way to get him back. Tomorrow we'll come up with a plan."

Looking down at her outrageous red dress and come-get-me shoes, B. J. felt like a woman waking from a bad dream. First she'd tried to turn herself into an outdoors type and then she'd tried to turn herself into a vamp.

"I'm through with plans, Maxie. I'm through playing games. From now on, I'm going to be myself."

SEVENTEEN

Crash sat up all night thinking about what to do next. By dawn he knew that there was only one thing to do. The only problem was, it involved more people than just himself.

He climbed aboard his Harley and set out to his brother's house.

"You look like hell," Joe said, holding wide the door. "Come on in."

Walking into Joe's house was always like walking into a museum. Everything looked old, well preserved, and cataloged, expensive antiques from France and England, ancient handwoven rugs from Persia, priceless jade statues from China. Even this early in the morning, there was not a piece of furniture, not a knick-knack, not a doodad out of place.

Crash always entered carefully, feeling like the proverbial bull in a china shop.

Today was no different. He leaned against the mantel to keep from having to sit in the chair.

"Does anybody even live here?" he said.

"I'll ignore that crack." Joe nodded toward a wing chair. "Have a seat."

"I don't want to wrinkle the cushion."

"For Pete's sake." Joe tossed the cushion onto the floor. "Sit down before you fall down. Now, tell me what's wrong."

Now that he was there, Crash had cold feet. "Didn't sleep, that's all."

Joe checked his watch. "Let me get this straight. You got me up at six o'clock on Sunday morning to tell me about your insomnia."

"Yeah, I guess I did."

"What do I look like? Somebody who rolled off a watermelon truck?"

Joe was a perfect brother, supportive without being pushy, concerned without being dictatorial, unfailingly kind. Not only that, he was Crash's best friend. Always had been, always would be.

There are times in a man's life when he has to trust somebody, and that somebody happened to be sitting across the room from Crash, his hair tousled from the night's sleep, his cheeks covered with beard stubble, and his socks on wrong side out.

"It all started with a woman," Crash said.

"Aha." Joe made a steeple of his fingers. "Would it be the woman in red?"

"Who she is doesn't matter. What happened does."

"What happened?"

"I don't quite know myself."

"Take your time. This is not a court of law."

"Spoken like a jackass."

"Finally, the baby brother I know and love."

Joe went into the kitchen and came back with two cups of coffee and a plate of English muffins. Crash smiled ruefully.

"My brother, the unflappable genius. You're always prepared, aren't you, Joe?"

"Eat your muffin, Nat."

They ate awhile in silence. Over coffee Crash worked up enough courage to get to the point.

"That's a drastic solution," Joe said after Crash had finished explaining his plans.

"Drastic situations require drastic solutions." He strapped on his helmet. "Besides, if you don't keep moving, you die."

Joe clapped his hand on his brother's shoulder. "Take care, Nat."

"Same to you. . . . I'll be back to dance at your wedding, but I hope it's not to that mannequin."

"Nat . . ."

"Okay, okay." When he was astride his Harley he gave a salute. "See you around, Joe."

"Crash, wait."

Joe hurried over to the motorcycle, concern written all over him.

"Are you sure about all this?"

"How can a man be sure about anything?"

Joe studied the two mockingbirds in the giant magnolia that presided over his flower garden.

He was not one to make hasty judgments or hasty decisions. Ask anybody who knew him, especially his fiancée. She'd been trying for months to pin him down on a wedding date.

"Nat, you know I'd do anything in the world for you. Why don't you stick around for a while, think things through. I'll help you out any way I can."

"Thanks, Joe. A man's gotta do what a man's gotta do."

Joe was thoughtful another long while, drumming his fingers against the Harley and studying the fountain nestled among his roses.

"You already told me you don't want to discuss the woman, and I don't mean to delve into your personal problems." Joe cleared his throat. "The trail to the altar is long and fairly arduous, but I've made it this far. I don't deem myself an expert, but I might be of assistance with this matter of the heart."

"I'm afraid it's too late for that, Joe. I've already messed things up royally. Besides, the lady and I don't see eye to eye on anything except a dog." Crash fastened his helmet, then saluted. "See you when I see you, pal."

His brother hugged him close.

"Maybe I'm not such a hotshot in the love department—it's a common failure among the Beauregard men. But I do know this. Running away from problems is not the answer."

Crash thought about his farm and his legal degree

and his Harley and the big wide world outside Tupelo. A fire burned in his soul, and all he knew was that he had to confront it and contain it or it would consume him.

"I'm not running away, Joe; I'm running *toward*."

EIGHTEEN

Her case file was open on her desk, the one she secretly called "The Rabbit Who Ate Tupelo." Her reception area was empty, her office was empty, her conference room was empty.

B. J. took out a yellow legal pad and made a list of things to do. She wrote "hire legal secretary" at the head of her list. Next she wrote "client contacts," but her heart wasn't in it. Her heart was still in Crash's country retreat, wounded and bleeding on his floor.

She made a little moaning sound, and Baxter licked her legs. In the hall, the antique clock she and Maxie had found at an auction bonged the lunch hour.

When she'd been living in Philadelphia she was often too busy to eat lunch. Dinner too. Sometimes she'd order in, but mostly she'd sit at her desk and work straight through.

"I've got to get busy or I'll never build that kind of practice in Tupelo," she said. Baxter was the only one there to hear, and he thumped his tail in what she considered an extremely intelligent and understanding manner.

"A power lunch. That's the ticket." She went to the closet in her office and took out a navy blazer. It was beginning to get hot in Mississippi, but B. J. knew the rules: To play the power game you had to dress the part.

She put on her blazer, tightened the pins in her French twist, then studied herself in the bathroom mirror. For all appearances she was exactly the same woman who had come to Tupelo weeks ago. On the outside she looked the same. It was the inside that felt different.

Her heart wasn't in power lunches, either. Her heart was lying crushed on Maxwell Street where Crash had left her three days earlier without even saying good-bye.

B. J. went to her break room and dug around in the refrigerator for some cucumbers. She didn't hear Maxie come in, didn't know her sister was in the room till she snatched the bag of cucumbers out of B. J.'s hand.

"Just as I thought," Maxie said.

"What?" B. J. felt defensive. Ever since her ill-fated evening of attempted seduction she'd been wanting to bite somebody's head off, and Maxie's would do. She snatched the cucumbers back. "Do you mind? That's my lunch."

"We're going somewhere that serves real food."

"Like what? Chocolate almond fudge with marshmallows on the top?" She jerked a chair out from the table and sat down. "No, thank you. I've had enough of your interference, Maxie. Go paint dragons on somebody's walls."

"I don't have to paint a dragon. She's sitting in my sister's chair."

B. J. took a vicious bite of her cucumber. "That's what happens when you turn into a dried-up old maid, Maxie. You start breathing fire and brimstone."

Maxie sailed her sassy sailor hat onto the table, then straddled a chair facing her sister.

"I suppose it'll be orthopedic shoes and a walking cane next."

"Probably. Who cares?"

Maxie peeled a cucumber, then began to munch.

"These aren't bad," she said.

"I told you."

"Big sister knows best?"

"Yes." B. J. didn't believe a word she said, but she said it anyhow. She had to get her life back together, and lying was as good a place to start as any.

Maxie grabbed another cucumber. "That's some example you're setting. I hate to think that in a few years all I have to look forward to is lunching alone on a bag of cucumbers."

"I'm not alone."

"You were until I came along."

"I have Baxter."

"Baxter needs a daddy."

"Maxie, don't even start."

"Okay." Maxie poured two glasses of water. "By

the way, do you have any idea where Judge Nathaniel Bridge Beauregard is?"

"I haven't asked. I don't want to know." B. J. had a sudden vision of Crash bending over her on the rug. She saw him, felt him, tasted him. "Why do you ask? Has he gone somewhere?"

"Word on the street this morning is that he's hung up his robes."

"That's his style, I hear. Hang up the robes and take off on that Harley of his."

"For good," Maxie said.

"For good?"

"I got it straight from the chancery clerk's office at the courthouse."

When Stephen had left her at the altar, B. J. thought she knew the pain of loss. How wrong she'd been. What she'd felt then was nothing compared to the total devastation and complete isolation she felt now. Her heart was uprooted, her soul was lost, her whole world was in shambles.

"Mrs. Parker gave me these." She held the bag of cucumbers toward Maxie. It gave her something to hang onto.

Maxie tore a paper towel off the rack and handed it to B. J.

"Who is Mrs. Parker?"

"A client. The one with the wild rabbit." B. J. wiped her eyes, then blew her nose. "This is all she had to pay me with. When she set this little bag on my desk, I felt as if she'd given me a check for a million dollars."

Maxie knew when to keep quiet. She picked up the paring knife and a medium-sized cucumber. A pile of green peelings grew in the middle of the table as B. J. talked.

"I wasn't wearing a power suit the day she came to see me. I wasn't even wearing a jacket." She sniffed and dabbed at her eyes. "Do you know how it felt to use my skills to help somebody like that?"

"How did it feel, B. J.?"

"The way I imagined when I was twelve years old and trying out my litigation skills on the mules in Grandpa's barn." Dreams long forgotten bubbled to the surface, dreams of helping the downtrodden, the underdog. When had the dreams changed? When had dreams of helping to bring justice to the masses turned to dreams of getting the best cases, making the biggest scores?

She looked down at the paper bag on the table. When she'd brought it, Mrs. Parker had been wearing a faded chino dress with a frayed lace collar—her Sunday best.

"It felt the way practicing law ought to feel," B. J. said softly.

Looking down at her jacket, she added, "What's the temperature outside, Maxie?"

"Eighty."

"Too darned hot for this."

B. J. shucked her jacket and didn't even bother to hang it up. It slid off the back of the chair and landed on the floor. Baxter promptly dragged it off to his basket.

"Can this be the same woman who only moments ago was contemplating orthopedic shoes?" Maxie said.

B. J. raked the cucumber peelings off the table and put them into the garbage can. Then she looked down at herself and undid the top two buttons on her blouse.

"There . . . that's better."

"Atta girl." Maxie smiled at her. "You're going to find him, aren't you?"

B. J. remembered then, remembered the way he'd looked that night in his house . . . the fleck of gold in the center of his eyes, the shock of blond hair that always looked windblown as if he'd come down from some distant mountain peak, the gleam of sweat on his body, the slash of red across his left shoulder where her fingernails had dug in.

"*If* I love a woman . . ." he'd said.

"Yes, Maxie. I'm going to find him."

NINETEEN

Crash whistled while he made the corn bread. Not that he was merry. Not by a long shot. It's just that whistling filled up the silence. As many times as he'd been to the Smokies he'd never realized how the silence could get under a man's skin.

He poured the bread into a cast-iron skillet, poked his fire, then glanced across the way.

"Fool," he said to himself. "What did you expect to see?"

The campsite next to his was empty. There was no lopsided tent, no conglomeration of camping equipment, no stray mutt poking his nose out the tent flap. And most of all, no slender, long-legged woman with flashing eyes and a temper to match.

The sun dropped down behind the mountains, leaving a spectacular display of red and purple and gold in the west, and the corn bread sent forth a delicious aroma that made Crash's mouth water.

He tested the bread with the end of his finger. It was perfect.

"I'm getting good at this," he said.

He ate the whole pone, then took out his harmonica and sat with his back propped against the tent pole. A million stars popped into the sky, and a summer wind stirred the leaves of the branches of the pine trees so that they whispered secrets in the night.

It was a night made for love. Crash segued into a blues tune, then leaned back and watched the moon track across the dark sky while the haunting music washed over him. He played his entire repertoire of blues, played until the moon hung low and the stars began to fade, played until he was so sleepy, he knew he would fall into his bag and never blink until morning.

A cold wet nose woke him up.

"What . . ."

Disoriented, he opened his eyes and saw three things: a high-flying sun, a little dog's furry face, and Philadelphia. The sight of all three blinded him.

"I need some help with my tent," she said.

Struck dumb by the sight of her, he lay in his bag squinting at her.

She was no longer dressed in red. Her shorts were cutoff jeans, faded and frayed, her blouse was pink, unbuttoned at the top, and her shoes looked as if they'd been hiked in a few times. Not exactly the kind of dress a woman wears when she's bent on seduction. Still, with Philadelphia you never knew.

He felt as if somebody had slammed a sledgehammer against his heart. She loved him. That was his first and most natural thought. He'd gone through life with a wink and a smile, and love came to him as naturally as rivers flow into the ocean.

"Philadelphia!" he said, ready to leap from his sleeping bag and embrace her.

Then he remembered her perfidy, remembered that she wasn't one of the Beauregards, who in spite of being the most driven people in the world still knew how to let love show.

Though Crash never erred on the side of caution, he figured it was the only way to protect his bruised and battered heart.

"That's a strange request coming from a woman who prides herself on being self-sufficient."

"Maybe I'm not as self-sufficient as I thought."

"What? You admit there are some things you can't do all by yourself?"

"You're making this hard."

Their first meeting flashed before him, and he gave her a wicked grin.

"Not yet," he said, "but it's getting there."

She whirled around and stalked off. He knew the exact minute she changed her mind. She squared her shoulders, lifted her head, stuck out her elbows, and made a sharp about-face.

"I ought to have my head examined," she muttered.

Crash was beginning to enjoy himself. He sat up

buck naked, the sleeping bag crumpled in his lap and the sun on his back. Baxter licked his face.

"Come here, old boy. Tell me how much you missed me. Tell me what an irresistible guy I am." Crash put the little dog in his lap and rubbed his fur.

"I wouldn't go that far," Philadelphia said.

She flushed and looked as if she didn't quite know what to do with herself. Crash decided to let her squirm, but only for a little while.

In spite of everything he still loved her. He'd known that when he left Tupelo. And now, seeing her in the place where they'd first met, he felt love so strongly, he wanted to shout it to the mountaintops.

But what about Philadelphia? Did she feel anything or was she just playing games?

"How far would you go?" he asked, softly.

She looked into the distance at the mountains, the exuberant colors of spring metamorphosed into the rich and full greens of summer. She looked soft and vulnerable.

"All the way from Tupelo to the Smokies," she said.

"Why?"

"To apologize."

Disappointment washed through him. Apologies were nice, but admissions of a grander sort were better. Why didn't she say something he could pin his hopes on, something like, "I've never met a man like you, Crash," or "You turn me on," or even "I really wanted you to be the father of my child, Crash. Only you."

Or even something old-fashioned like, "I love you."

"You could have sent me a letter," he said. "I read."

"I didn't know if they delivered mail here."

So . . . she really would have sent him a letter. Crash nuzzled Baxter's soft fur while he thought about Philadelphia sitting in her business suit and pearls writing him a stiff and formal little apology.

"How did you know where to find me?"

"Joseph. I went to his office and begged."

It was hard to think of Philadelphia lowering herself to ask his whereabouts, let alone begging.

"Really?" he said, barely containing his smile.

"Almost. Your brother is extremely protective. But he came through when I explained why I wanted to see you."

He could picture that scene, staid and steady Joseph shaken to the core when Philadelphia explained how she'd tried to trick Crash, then how she'd had a change of heart and wanted to tell him that all along she'd loved him and she was sorry she hadn't told him so in the first place.

"Joe's a big believer in apologies. He must have turned three shades of red, though, when you told him why."

"No. Actually he understood perfectly."

"He did?"

"Yes. He likes Baxter."

"Baxter?"

Hearing his name, Baxter bounced around, nipping at their feet and barking. The only trouble was, he didn't know who to go to. They were both calling his name.

Crash scooped him up and scratched his ears. It

gave him something to do while he was trying to sort his mixed emotions.

"What does Baxter have to do with this?" he said.

"I came to apologize for depriving Baxter of his daddy."

"You didn't come to say you're sorry about trying to use me for stud service?"

"No . . . I'm not sorry about that."

She didn't crack a smile, and she certainly didn't look remorseful. As a matter of fact, her face was sewed up tighter than Dick's hat band. In the courtroom, her opponents must have shuddered in their boots.

Crash wasn't exactly shuddering, but he was confused . . . and getting mad. He wanted to play for keeps, and she was still playing games.

"A little remorse might become you," he said.

"Become *me*!"

She turned red in the face, and her eyes shot fire. Finally he'd gotten a reaction from her.

"What about *you*, you bullheaded back of a mule?"

"I've done nothing to be remorseful about."

"Ha! That'll be the day." She jerked Baxter out of his grasp. "I'm sorry I ever came looking for you . . . and I'm certainly sorry I ever asked for your help. Don't you come near my tent."

"What about Baxter? He needs his daddy."

"Why don't you try whistling? Maybe he'll come running . . . but not if I have anything to do with it."

She stalked off, magnificent in her rage. Baxter twisted and turned in her grip, whining and looking back at Crash. His paws scrabbled along her side, and out of her pocket flew a neatly folded piece of yellow paper.

Crash scooped it up and was about to call that she'd dropped something when the word at the top caught his eye: Baby. Riveted, he carried the note inside his tent and began to read.

TWENTY

"Arrogant . . . muleheaded . . . stubborn . . ."

B. J. kicked her rolled-up tent. Foolishly close to tears, she set Baxter down then rummaged into her pocket for a tissue.

"Where is anything when you need it?" She wiped her face with the back of her hands. "I will not cry . . . I will not cry . . ."

She'd been a fool to follow Crash to the mountains.

"Change his spots, indeed!" A man like Nathaniel Bridge Beauregard never changed his spots.

Glancing over her shoulder to be sure he wasn't watching, she sank onto her folded-up tent. He was probably in his own tent gloating.

Now what? If she turned around and went home, she'd be repeating an old pattern: lose and run.

She should have listened to Maxie.

"When you get there, for Pete's sake, don't let your

pride get in the way," she said, standing beside B. J.'s car just before she started her journey of the heart.

"What pride? I'd call what I'm planning to do nothing short of groveling."

"There's nothing groveling about telling a man you love him. Just tell him you love him, B. J."

But had she listened? No. She'd marched over there like Sherman storming Atlanta and told him she wanted help with her tent. She was a coward, that's what. She was afraid he wouldn't love her back.

Baxter nosed her legs, and she pulled him close. "What if he doesn't love me back?" she whispered.

Baxter licked her wet face, and crazy as it seemed she felt better. She rummaged into her duffel bag for her instruction sheet, then unfolded the lump of canvas and set to work.

"Need any help?"

Crash's voice, as sweet and hot as molasses, scalded her skin. She closed her eyes, said a silent prayer for guidance, then turned to face him. Tarzan on a Harley, his leather pants molded to his legs, his shirt left carelessly unbuttoned, his smile wicked.

She was whisked back in time, face to face with the same delightful scoundrel she'd met and fallen in love with on this very mountain. Except . . . he wasn't the same. Something about him was different.

Then she noticed his hair. He'd dampened it with water and tried to tame it, with mixed results. It lay behind his ears, then kicked up along the curve of his neck and around his temples.

She'd never seen a more endearing sight in her life. B. J. almost cried.

Instead, she clutched a tent pole to her chest. "I don't think so. The tent may prove a little ornery, but I think I can handle it."

"I see. What I don't see is what brought you to these mountains in the first place."

He dismounted, then leaned against his big chrome-and-metal stallion.

"I thought a big-city girl like you hated the outdoors."

"Maybe the big-city girl has decided to change her style."

"Sort of like the animal who changed its stripes?"

He was referring to himself, of course. Though, if he'd changed his stripes she had yet to see the different color. Nathaniel Bridge "Crash" Beauregard was still the handsome, devil-may-care vagabond she knew . . . and loved.

"Sort of," she said.

And then because he looked at her a certain way, because it was impossible to ignore the starlight in the center of his eyes, she told him the truth.

At least, as much as she could manage at one time. She'd always depended on herself. Sharing bits and pieces of her life with somebody else was hard.

"I've done some soul-searching." The light in his eyes almost blinded her. "About the way I've been living."

"All work and no play?"

"You might say that."

Caught in the net of their own desires, they stared at each other, hungry but gun-shy. If she'd been in a courtroom, B. J. would have thought of a dozen ways to end the impasse. But they were in the Smokies, where the only rules were those of nature.

"My offer still stands," Crash said finally. "But I'm not talking about the tent."

"You're not?"

"I'm talking about this."

He pulled a note from his pocket. Her list. The one she'd so painstakingly made on her yellow legal pad. She kicked herself for being the kind of woman who had to organize her thoughts on paper.

"Is this the truth?" he said, holding the note out.

It was all there, her list of Crash's assets as a father, the list of characteristics she wanted him to pass on to her baby, even a list of things she'd need when the baby was born. Around the borders of the paper she'd drawn hearts with wings, and at the bottom, written in red, "Because I love him, only him."

Now was the time to take Maxie's advice: "Take the risk and the angels come." Angels might not come, but there was only one way to find out.

"Yes. It's the truth."

He closed in on her like a storm that had been building all summer. Taking the tent pole from her hand, he scooped her up and held her close.

"What are you doing?" she said.

"I'm planning to help you with that little project."

Giving her a wonderfully wicked grin, he marched toward his tent.

"Are you kidnapping me?"

"Yes. Are you complaining?"

"No."

He elbowed aside the tent flap. "Let's get one thing straight before we go in."

"What's that?"

"This baby will be mine too. Legally."

"Is that a proposal?"

"Lawyers . . . always wanting to dot every *i* and cross every *t*."

"Well, is it? Because if it is, I want you on bended knee."

"One or both?"

"Both."

"I think I can arrange that."

Inside he stripped aside his clothes, then undressed her slowly.

"Stand right there, Philadelphia. Don't move."

"How can I move? I can hardly breathe."

He dropped to his knees and buried his face in her soft secret places. Sensations of purest love shot upward, and she knew their baby would have the greatest gift of all: being conceived in love. She wove her fingers in his hair and pulled him close. He had magic lips and a tongue of flame, and she spun into a wonderland, burning, burning, crying out her pleasure again and again.

Crash looked up at her, smiling. "You like that, don't you?"

"I love it. . . . I love *you*."

"And I love you. Did I fail to mention that?"

"Yes, but I'll see that it doesn't happen again."

Still on his knees, he drew her down, then cupped her face.

"I never knew being in love would be so wonderful," he said, and the wonder he felt was in his kiss, in the way he bent over her, in the way he held her.

The flames he'd kindled leaped to life once more. He pressed against her, strong and powerful and urgent.

"I want you," she whispered. "All of you."

"You have me, Philadelphia . . . now and forever."

Still on his knees, he took her from behind, each thrust an affirmation of love, each strangled pleasure-cry a declaration straight from his heart. He was the sun, the moon, the stars, and she spiraled upward, spinning, spinning in his orbit.

"Now?" His whisper was hoarse, urgent. "Now?"

"Yes . . . Oh, yes . . . Now."

Gripping the canvas floor, she took him fully, completely for the final frenzied ride. And when he spewed his seed, she knew she had found what she'd been looking for: She'd found heaven.

For a moment he rested his face against her back, and it was not until he turned her gently over and laid her on the floor that she saw the dampness on his cheeks. She caught his tears with her fingertips, then brought her fingers into her mouth and licked them away.

Still on his knees, he smiled at her. "Will you marry me, Philadelphia?"

Sometimes, suddenly, you see your future, and it's so remarkable a mere glimpse makes your heart hurt. Momentarily struck by her vision, Philadelphia pressed her hand over her heart.

"Will you?" he whispered, bending over her.

Overflowing with love, she cupped his face.

"Does this mean I get to ride into the sunset on the back of a Harley?"

"Yes. I think it's the best way to go."

"So do I, Crash . . . so do I."

EPILOGUE

Two months later

The sun dropped behind the stand of oak and pine trees, and from deep inside the woods a whippoorwill called. A breeze set the wind chimes on the front porch tinkling. Sitting side by side on the wicker swing, B. J. and Nat looked at each other and burst out laughing.

There was an answering sound from beside the front porch, a plaintive "maaa." Beneath the sign that proclaimed Beauregard and Beauregard, Attorneys at Law, was a small billy goat.

"Well, Philadelphia, what do you think of our latest paycheck?"

B. J. pretended to assess the goat with an expert eye.

"He looks a little skinny, Crash. Are you sure we should accept a skinny goat for saving Mr. Sims's pet rabbit from the stew pot?"

"Do you think we should have held out for a fat one?"

"Hmmm." B. J. left the swing and went down the steps to inspect the goat. "I think this calls for a consultation, Counselor."

"By all means, Counselor." Crash unfolded his long legs, stretched lazily, then joined her beside the goat. "Which boardroom do you suggest we use?"

"I'm rather partial to the one upstairs. . . . The one with the brass bed and the patchwork quilt."

He nuzzled her neck. "You know how to take a man's mind off his business, don't you?"

"I try."

"I was thinking of our other boardroom." Crash untied the billy goat. "The one with the hay."

"You have the *best* ideas."

They led the little billy to the barn and put him in his very own stable with plenty of hay and a donkey in the stall beside him for company. After they'd patted him and assured him there was a big, wide pasture outside for his comfort and pleasure, they adjourned up the ladder to the hayloft.

"Philadelphia, do you want to call this meeting to order, or shall I?"

"Let me." She gave him an arch smile. "Besides, I have an agenda."

"An agenda? If you're going to get all that fancy we'll have to start billing our clients for two goats instead of one."

"Or maybe even a whole cow."

"You're darned right."

"Sit still now. This meeting is about to come to order." B. J. unbuttoned his shirt and ran her hands over his chest.

"Hmmm, I like the way you handle things, Mrs. Beauregard."

"Lately I've had lots of practice." She unzipped his pants, then bent down and took him in her mouth.

"I hope this is going to be a very long meeting."

She lifted her head, smiling. "Oh, it will be, Counselor. Rest assured. It will be a *very* long meeting."

She pushed him down into the hay, then sprawled on top of him. Crash reached under her full denim skirt and found what he wanted.

"So slick," he murmured. "So hot . . ." He shifted, impaling her. "I love it when you're ready for me."

"I'm always ready for you." She began to move in the age-old rhythm that took his breath away. "The first item on my agenda is a goat cart," she said, breathless and flushed.

Crash thrust powerfully, then caught her hips and held her fast.

"Good idea, Philadelphia. But then, you're full of good ideas."

"I'm certainly full of one now. . . . The best of all."

"You wicked, wanton wench. Have I told you lately that I love you?"

"Is that a song?"

"Yes, it's music . . . and so is this."

He flipped her over, caught her hands above her head, then took them on a wild and frenzied journey that made conversation impossible. Sensation after sensation rocked B. J., and she wondered how it was possible to be so richly blessed. Every day with Crash was better than the one before.

From the moment she'd committed herself to him in the mountains, then ridden off on the back of his Harley to find a justice of the peace to make it legal, she'd felt as if she'd sprouted wings. Each day brought a new discovery, a new sense of freedom, a new wonder.

The scent of sweet hay filled her nostrils, the sound of her husband's ragged breathing filled her ears, and love filled her heart. Crash cried out her name, and they exploded together. A million tiny stars fell from the sky and scattered through her body, and she knew that she would feel their glow for a lifetime . . . and beyond.

He stretched on top of her, languorous and smiling, taking the bulk of his weight on his elbows.

"What's next on the agenda, Counselor?"

She gave him a wicked grin. "More of the same."

"That's what I was hoping." Already he could feel the need for her rising again.

"But first, there is one important item we need to discuss."

"I'm all ears."

"No, you're not." She touched him, grinning.

"Like I said, you sure know how to handle a meeting. So, tell me this important item, but make it fast because I'm raring to get back to the major agenda."

"A goat cart," she said.

"For Baxter?"

Baxter loved riding in the sidecar on the Harley. Crash figured he'd be equally pleased with his very own goat cart.

"He can ride too."

"Too? Did you say *too?*"

"I did."

Her smile was so big, she thought her face would break. When the truth dawned, Crash was awestruck. Tenderly, he placed a hand over her abdomen.

"Does this mean what I think it means?" he whispered.

"Yes. You remember that little project we started in the mountains?"

"How could I forget?"

"We were successful," she whispered.

He sat up and treated her midsection to a tender and thorough exploration with hands and mouth. And after he'd finished, he parted her thighs and slid into her soft, welcoming folds once more.

"We'd better make sure," he said.

Eight months later

The hospital corridor was all white and a mile long. Or so it seemed to Maxie. She was a nervous wreck.

The call she'd been waiting for for weeks had finally come.

"It's a boy," Crash had said. "A seven-pound baby boy."

Maxie was so excited, she put her skirt on backward. When she finally got her skirt right, she discovered that she buttoned her blouse up wrong. Now, rushing down the long corridor to see her nephew, she realized she was wearing one pink shoe and one red. Furthermore, she'd grabbed her turquoise linen jacket instead of the green. With her red hair caught up in an orange ribbon, she looked like a walking neon sign.

She shifted the giant panda bear she was holding and raced full tilt down the hall.

"Might as well get used to it, squirt," she said, already talking to the nephew she was rushing to meet. "That's the way Aunt Maxie is, topsy-turvy clothes and a brain to match. . . . Whoops!"

She smacked into a solid, immovable object. Her panda bear flew upward, and Maxie flew backward, arms and legs flailing. She would have fallen if a large pair of arms hadn't caught her.

"Gotcha."

Dazed, she looked up into the face of Mr. Perfect. She'd have swooned if she hadn't already been in a virtual faint.

The man holding her changed his expression from concern to faint recognition.

"Maxie?"

"That's right. Magic Maxie."

"Joseph Beauregard," he said needlessly, which just went to prove that he was as flustered as she.

Bent over backward on the arms of a dark and handsome hero, she felt like a heroine in a silent movie. Suddenly she started to giggle.

"I forgot to shave," he said.

She laughed harder.

"I don't see that it's all that funny. I'm planning to stop at the barber's on my way to the office."

"Good grief, Joseph. I'm not laughing at your beard shadow, I'm laughing at us. We must look like a pair of silver-screen lovers."

You'd think she had shot him from a cannon. That's how fast he straightened up. She reached down to retrieve her fallen panda, and collided with him again.

"Oops, sorry," she said. "I was just getting my bear."

"I thought that was my bear."

They both turned around, and on the floor behind them was another giant panda, a twin to the one Maxie had bought for her nephew.

"It seems we think alike," he said.

"Good heavens, I hope not."

He arched an eyebrow at her, then they jerked up their separate pandas and hurried toward room 314, not speaking. At the door they both paused, brought to a dead halt by the sight of Nat bending over the bed where B. J. lay holding a tiny bundle of blue.

"Maxie . . . Joe." He beamed at them. "Come in here and meet our son." He gently lifted the baby and folded back the blanket so they could see his tiny face, as red and wrinkled as a peach pit. "Joe, meet your uncle Joe and your aunt Maxie."

"Joe?" His brother beamed. "You named him for me?"

"Great Caesar in a goat cart. What did you expect? You're my hero."

"Don't let him sweet talk you, Joe," B. J. said, holding out her hands and offering her cheek for her brother-in-law's kiss. "Before you know it you'll be agreeing to everything he asks of you."

"I'm used to pulling Nat's irons out of the fire. What is it this time?"

Crash came around the side of the bed and placed the baby in Aunt Maxie's waiting arms. Then he looped an arm around her and the other around his brother.

"Get ready," B. J. said, smiling. "Here it comes."

"I want the two of you to be the godparents."

"I can't believe it," Maxie said. "Good grief. I think I'm going to cry." B. J. pulled a tissue from the box beside her bed and handed it to her sister. "I never cry. B. J.'s always the one."

"I'm honored," Joe said, his face as solemn as a judge. "Absolutely honored."

In one of her typical Maxie flashes, she changed from tears to laughter.

"Do you know what this means?" Leaning around her brother-in-law, she addressed Joe.

"We stand up at the christening," he said.

"Yes, but even better, we get to plan the *party*." Maxie offered her finger, and the baby latched on with a grip that meant business. She cooed at him. "We're going to plan you the best party in the whole world. Yes, we are."

Joe cleared his throat. "Something quiet and sedate at the country club might be appropriate," he said hopefully.

"Quiet and sedate!" Maxie leaned close to the baby and crooned. "You're not going to be that kind of boy, are you? No, you're not."

She turned back to Joe. "I know a man who has *real* zebras."

"Real zebras?" Joe began to look alarmed.

"Yes." Maxie's red ponytail bounced in her excitement. "He might even be able to get us a real tiger."

Joe ran a hand under his collar. "Perhaps a stuffed tiger or two would be appropriate for the decorations."

"Stuffed? Good grief."

Maxie handed the baby back to his daddy, then linked her arm through Joe's and propelled him from the room.

"We need to talk."

"I have an appointment."

"What could you possibly have that's more important than your nephew's christening party?"

As the godmother led the godfather through the door, they heard her say, "If we don't launch this kid right, he's liable to grow up to be a stuffed shirt."

Crash grinned at his wife.

"What do you think, Philadelphia? Will Joey get real tigers or stuffed ones?"

"I guess we'll have to wait and see."

She held out her hand, and Crash leaned over to kiss her.

"I can think of a few things to do while we're waiting," he whispered.

"Will I like them?"

"Every one. And that's a promise."

THE EDITORS'
CORNER

It's hot in the city! And in the country. And in
the North. And in the South. And in the mountains.
And at the seashore. And . . . well, you get the picture. It's just plain hot! Don't worry though, Loveswept's September loot of books will match the
sultry weather out there. Even the air conditioner
won't stop these characters from sizzling right off
the pages and into your homes!

Devlin Sinclair and Gabrielle Rousseau are walking **ON THIN ICE**, LOVESWEPT #850, Eve
Gaddy's novel about two attorneys bent on taking on
the world and each other. Thrown together through
no wish of their own, Devlin and Gabrielle must de-
fend a reputed crime boss—a case that could ultimately make their careers, involving a man who
could ultimately ruin Gabrielle's life. Devlin knew
there was more to his sinfully gorgeous partner, es-

pecially since he accidentally bumped into her in the Midnight and Lace Lingerie shop! Annoyed that Devlin looked as if he'd guessed her wildest secrets, Gabrielle had to struggle not to melt when the charming rogue called her beautiful. But sometimes, in the heat of denial, one can discover heat of another kind. Eve Gaddy's romantic adventure pairs a fallen angel with a man who's her match in all things sensual and judicial!

In **AFTERGLOW,** LOVESWEPT #851 by Loveswept favorite Faye Hughes, professional treasure hunter Sean Kilpatrick is about to meet her match when she joins forces with Dalton Gregory in the search for a legendary cache of gold, silver, and priceless jewels buried somewhere on Gregory land. When Dalton comes to town to oust Sean, who he's sure is just a slick huckster on the make, he finds a copper-haired beauty whose enthusiasm for the project quickly becomes infectious. Sean is stunned by her intense attraction to this gorgeous, yet conservative history professor, but when he agrees to help chase a fortune, close quarters may not be all that they share. Spending more time together only accentuates the slow burn that is raging into a steady afterglow. Faye Hughes tempts readers with the ultimate treasure hunt in a tantalizingly steamy romantic romp!

Cheryln Biggs tells a deliciously unpredictable tale about the **GUNSLINGER'S LADY,** LOVESWEPT #852. There's a new girl in town in Tombstone, Arizona, and Jack Ringo aims to find out just what she's doing sprawled in his cactus patch dressed up in petticoats—especially since the Old West Festival doesn't start until tomorrow! Kate Holliday can't understand why Johnny Ringo is dressed up in strange clothes and without his guns, but the man was definitely as dangerously handsome as ever! Jack is quickly bewitched by Kate's mystery, frustrated at her existence, and inflamed by the heated passion of a woman who may disappear with the dawn. Adrift in a world she'd never imagined, uncertain of all but one man's need, can a sassy adventuress find her future in the arms of a man who couldn't guarantee the coming of tomorrow? Cheryln Biggs delivers a timeless love story that dabbles in destiny and breaks all the rules!

Loveswept newcomer Pat Van Wie adds to our lineup of delectable September romances **RUNNING FOR COVER**, LOVESWEPT #853. When Deputy Marshal Kyle Munroe shows up at Jennifer Brooks's classroom door complete with an entourage, Jenny knows that her time of peace and security is long gone. Jenny is reluctant to trust the man who had once shunned all she had to offer, but deep down she knows that Kyle may very well be the only one she can truly count on. Threats against her father's life also put hers in danger and the reluctant pair go into hiding . . . until betrayal catapults them into a desperate flight. And once again, Kyle and Jenny are faced with the same decisions, whether to find safety and love together, or shadows and sadness apart. Sizzling with sexual tension and the breathless thrill of love on the run, Pat Van Wie's first Loveswept explores the joy and heartache of a desire too strong to subdue.

Happy reading!

With warmest regards,

Shauna Summers Joy Abella

Shauna Summers   Joy Abella

Editor   Administrative Editor

P.S. Look for these Bantam women's fiction titles coming in August. *New York Times* bestseller Tami Hoag's breathtakingly sensual novel, **DARK PARADISE,** is filled with heart-stopping suspense and shocking passion. Marilee Jennings is drawn to a man as hard and untamable as the land he loves, and to a town steeped in secrets—where a killer lurks. Another *New York Times* bestselling author, Betina Krahn, is back with **THE MERMAID,** a tale of a woman ahead of her time and an academic who must decide if he will risk everything he holds dear to side with the Lady Mermaid. Dubbed the queen of romantic adventure by *Affaire de Coeur*, Katherine O'Neal returns with **BRIDE OF DANGER,** her most spellbinding—and irresistible—novel yet! Night after night, Mylene charmed the secrets out of men's souls, and not one suspected that she was a spy devoted to the cause of freedom. Until the evening she came face-to-face with the mysterious Lord Whitney, a man who will ask her to betray everything she's ever believed in. And immediately following this page, preview the Bantam women's fiction titles on sale in July.

Don't miss these extraordinary books
by your favorite Bantam authors

On sale in July:

THE SILVER ROSE
by Jane Feather

A PLACE TO CALL HOME
by Deborah Smith

The newest novel in the enthralling,
passionate Charm Bracelet Trilogy . . .

"Jane Feather is an accomplished
storyteller . . . rare and wonderful."
—*Daily News of Los Angeles*

THE SILVER ROSE
by Jane Feather
author of *The Diamond Slipper*

*Like the rose in the haunting tale of "Beauty and the
Beast," a silver rose on a charm bracelet brings together a
young woman and a battle-scarred lord . . . Ariel
Ravenspeare has been taught to loathe the earl of
Hawkesmoor and everything he represents. Their two
families have been sworn enemies for generations. But it's
one thing to hate him, and another to play the part
her vicious brothers have written for her—trapping
Hawkesmoor into a marriage that will destroy him, using
herself as bait. Forced into the marriage, Ariel will find
her new husband unexpectedly difficult to manipulate, as
well as surprisingly—and powerfully—attractive. But
beneath the passion lurks the strand of a long-hidden
secret . . . a secret embodied in a sparkling silver rose.*

Ranulf stood at the door to the Great Hall. He stared
out over the thronged courtyard, and when he saw
Ariel appear from the direction of the stables, he de-

scended the steps and moved purposefully toward her. She was weaving her way through the crowd, the dogs at her heels, a preoccupied frown on her face.

"Just where the hell have you been?" Ranulf demanded in a low voice, grabbing her arm above the elbow. The dogs growled but for once he ignored them. "How dare you vanish without a word to anyone! Where have you been? Answer me!" He shook her arm. The dogs growled again, a deep-throated warning. Ranulf turned on them with a foul oath, but he released his hold.

"Why should it matter where I've been?" Ariel answered. "I'm back now."

"Dressed like some homespun peasant's wife," her brother gritted through compressed lips. "Look at you. You had money to clothe yourself properly for your bridal celebrations, and you go around in an old riding habit that looks as if it's been dragged through a haystack. And your boots are worn through."

Ariel glanced down at her broadcloth skirts. Straw and mud clung to them, and her boots, while not exactly worn through, were certainly shabby and unpolished. She had been so uncomfortable dressing under the amused eye of her bridegroom that morning that she had grabbed what came to hand and given no thought to the occasion.

"I trust you have passed a pleasant morning, my wife." Simon's easy tones broke into Ranulf's renewed diatribe. The earl of Hawkesmoor had approached through the crowd so quietly that neither Ranulf nor his sister had noticed him. Ariel looked up with a flashing smile that betrayed her relief at his interruption.

"I went for a drive in the gig. Forgive me for

staying out overlong, but I drove farther than I'd thought to without noticing the time."

"Aye, it's a fine way to do honor to your husband," Ranulf snapped. "To appear clad like a serving wench who's been rolling in the hay. I'll not have it said that the earl of Ravenspeare's sister goes about like a tavern doxy—"

"Oh, come now, Ravenspeare!" Simon again interrupted Ranulf's rising tirade. "You do even less honor to your name by reviling your sister so publicly." Ariel flushed to the roots of her hair, more embarrassed by her husband's defense than by her brother's castigation.

"Your wife's appearance does not reflect upon the Hawkesmoor name, then?" Ranulf's tone was full of sardonic mockery. "But perhaps Hawkesmoors are less nice in their standards."

"From what I've seen of your hospitality so far, Ravenspeare, I take leave to doubt that," Simon responded smoothly, not a flicker of emotion in his eyes. He turned to Ariel, who was still standing beside him, wrestling with anger and chagrin. "However, I take your point, Ravenspeare. It is for a husband to correct his wife, not her brother.

"You are perhaps a little untidy, my dear. Maybe you should settle this matter by changing into a habit that will reflect well upon both our houses. I am certain the shooting party can wait a few minutes."

Ariel turned and left without a word. She kept her head lowered, her hood drawn up to hide her scarlet cheeks. It was one of her most tormenting weaknesses. Her skin was so fair and all her life she had blushed at the slightest provocation, sometimes even without good reason. She was always mortified at her obvious embarrassment, and the situation would be impossibly magnified.

Why had Simon interfered? Ranulf's insulting rebukes ran off her like water on oiled leather. By seeming to take her part, the Hawkesmoor had made a mountain out of a molehill. But then, he hadn't really taken her part. He had sent her away to change as if she were a grubby child appearing unwashed at the dinner table.

However, when she took a look at herself in the glass in her chamber, she was forced to admit that both men had had a point. Her hair was a wind-whipped tangle, her face was smudged with dust from her drive through the Fen blow, and her old broadcloth riding habit was thick with dust, the skirts caked with mud. But she'd had more important matters to attend to than her appearance, she muttered crossly, tugging at buttons and hooks.

Clad in just her shift, she washed her face and sponged her arms and neck, before letting down her hair. Throwing it forward over her face, she bent her head low and began to brush out the tangles. She was still muttering to herself behind the honeyed curtain when her husband spoke from the door.

"Your brothers' guests grow restless. I don't have much skill as a ladies' maid but perhaps I can help you."

Ariel raised her head abruptly, tossing back the glowing mane of hair. Her cheeks were pink with her efforts with the hairbrush and a renewed surge of annoyance.

The hounds greeted the new arrival with thumping tails. Their mistress, however, regarded the earl with a fulminating glare. "I have no need of assistance, my lord. And it's very discourteous to barge into my chamber without so much as a knock."

"Forgive me, but the door was ajar." His tone carelessly dismissed her objection. He closed the door on his words and surveyed her with his crooked little smile. "Besides, a wife's bedchamber is usually not barred to her husband."

"So you've already made clear, my lord," Ariel said tightly. "And I suppose it follows that a wife has no rights to privacy."

"Not necessarily." He limped forward and took the brush from her hand. "Sit." A hand on her shoulder pushed her down to the dresser stool. He began to draw the brush through the thick springy locks with strong, rhythmic strokes. "I've longed to do this since I saw you yesterday, waiting for me in the courtyard, with your hat under your arm. The sun was catching these light gold streaks in your hair. They're quite delightful." He lifted a strand that stood out much paler against the rich dark honey.

Ariel glanced at his face in the mirror. He was smiling to himself, his eyes filled with a sensual pleasure, his face, riven by the jagged scar, somehow softened as if this hair brushing were the act of a lover. She noticed how his hands, large and callused though they were, had an elegance, almost a delicacy to them. She had the urge to reach for those hands, to lay her cheek against them. A shiver ran through her.

"You're cold," he said immediately, laying down the brush. "The fire is dying." He turned to the hearth and with deft efficiency poked it back to blazing life, throwing on fresh logs. "Come now, you must make haste with your dressing before you catch cold." He limped to the armoire. "Will you wear the habit you wore yesterday? The crimson velvet suited you well." He drew out the garment as he spoke, and looked over at the sparse contents of the armoire. "You appear to have a very limited wardrobe, Ariel."

"I have little need of finery in the Fens," she stated, almost snatching the habit from him. "The life I lead doesn't lend itself to silks and velvets."

"The life you've led until now," he corrected thoughtfully, leaning against the bedpost, arms folded, as he watched her dress. "As the countess of Hawkesmoor, you will take your place at court, and in county society, I trust. The Hawkesmoors have always been active in our community of the Fens."

Unlike the lords of Ravenspeare. The local community was more inclined to hide from them than seek their aid. But neither of them spoke this shared thought.

Ariel fumbled with the tiny pearl buttons of her shirt. Her fingers were suddenly all thumbs. He sounded so assured, but she knew that she would never take her place at court or anywhere else as the wife of this man, whatever happened.

"Your hands must be freezing." He moved her fumbling fingers aside and began to slip the tiny buttons into the braided loops that fastened them. His hands brushed her breasts and her breath caught. His fingers stopped their work and she felt her nipples harden against the fine linen of her shift as goose bumps lifted on her skin. Then abruptly his hands dropped from her and he stepped back, his face suddenly closed.

She turned aside to pick up her skirt, stepping into it, fastening the hooks at her waist, trying to hide the trembling of her fingers, keeping her head lowered and averted until the hot flush died down on her creamy cheeks.

If only he would go away now. But he remained leaning against the bedpost.

She felt his eyes on her, following her every move, and that lingering sensuality in his gaze made her blood race. Even the simple act of pulling on her boots was invested with a curious voluptuousness under the intentness of his sea blue eyes. The man was ugly as sin, and yet she had never felt more powerfully attracted to anyone.

A new novel from one of the most
appealing voices in Southern fiction . . .

"A uniquely significant voice in contemporary
women's fiction."
—*Romantic Times*

A PLACE TO CALL HOME

by Deborah Smith

author of *Silk and Stone*

*Deborah Smith offers an irresistible Southern saga that
celebrates a sprawling, sometimes eccentric Georgia family
and the daughter at the center of their hearts. Twenty
years ago, Claire Maloney was the willful, pampered child
of the town's most respected family, but that didn't stop her
from befriending Roan Sullivan, a fierce, motherless boy
who lived in a rusted-out trailer amid junked cars. No
one in Dunderry—least of all Claire's family—could
understand the attraction. But Roan and Claire belonged
together . . . until the dark afternoon when violence and
terror overtook them and Roan disappeared from Claire's
life. Now, two decades later, Claire is adrift and the
Maloneys are still hoping the past can be buried under the
rich Southern soil . . .*

I planned to be the kind of old Southern lady who talks to her tomato plants and buys sweaters for her cats. I'd just turned thirty, but I was already sizing up where I'd been and where I was headed. So I knew that when I was old I'd be deliberately *peculiar*. I'd wear bright red lipstick and tell embarrassing true stories about my family, and people would say, "I heard she was always a little funny, if you know what I mean."

They wouldn't understand why, and I didn't intend to tell them. I thought I'd sit in a rocking chair on the porch of some fake-antebellum nursing home for decrepit journalists, get drunk on bourbon and Coca-Cola, and cry over Roan Sullivan. I was only ten the last time I saw him, and he was fifteen, and twenty years had passed since then, but I'd never forgotten him and knew I never would.

"I'd like to believe life turned out well for Roanie," Mama said periodically, and Daddy nodded without meeting her eyes, and they dropped the subject. They felt guilty about the part they'd played in driving Roan away, and they knew I couldn't forgive them for it. He was one of the disappointments between them and me, which was saying a lot, since I'd felt like such a helpless failure when they brought me home from the hospital last spring.

My two oldest brothers, Josh and Brady, didn't speak about Roan at all. They were away at college during most of the Roan Sullivan era in our family. But my two other brothers remembered him each time they came back from a hunting trip with a prize buck. "It can't hold a candle to the one Roan Sullivan shot when we were kids," Evan always said to Hop. "Nope," Hop agreed with a mournful sigh. "That buck was a king." Evan and Hop measured regret in terms of antlers.

As for the rest of the family—Daddy's side, Mama's side, merged halves of a family tree so large and complex and deeply rooted it looked like an overgrown oak to strangers—Roan Sullivan was only a fading reflection in the mirror of their biases and regrets and sympathies. How they remembered him depended on how they saw themselves and our world back then, and most of them had turned that painful memory to the wall.

But he and I were a permanent fixture in local history, as vivid and tragic as anything could be in a small Georgia community isolated in the lap of the mountains, where people hoard sad stories as carefully as their great-grandmothers' china. My great-grandmother's glassware and china service, by the way, were packed in a crate in Mama and Daddy's attic. Mama had this wistful little hope that I'd use it someday, that her only girl among five children would magically and belatedly blossom into the kind of woman who set a table with china instead of plastic.

There was hope for that. But what happened to Roan Sullivan and me changed my life and changed my family. Because of him we saw ourselves as we were, made of the kindness and cruelty that bond people together by blood, marriage, and time. I tried to save him and he ended up saving me. He might have been dead for twenty years—I didn't know then—but I knew I'd come full circle because of him: I would always wait for him to come back, too.

The hardest memories are the pieces of what might have been.

On sale in August:

DARK PARADISE
by Tami Hoag

THE MERMAID
by Betina Krahn

BRIDE OF DANGER
by Katherine O'Neal

The enchanting wit of *New York Times* bestseller

BETINA KRAHN

"Krahn has a delightful, smart touch."
—*Publishers Weekly*

THE PERFECT MISTRESS

___56523-0 $5.99/$7.99 Canada

THE LAST BACHELOR

___56522-2 $5.99/$7.50 Canada

THE UNLIKELY ANGEL

___56524-9 $5.99/$7.99 Canada
